Like a Love Song

Like a Love Song

GABRIELA MARTINS

Underlined

Text copyright © 2021 by Gabriela Martins
Cover art copyright © 2021 by Erick Davila

All rights reserved. Published in the United States by Underlined, an imprint of Random House Children's Books, a division of Penguin Random House LLC, New York.

Underlined is a registered trademark and the colophon is a trademark of Penguin Random House LLC.

GetUnderlined.com

Educators and librarians, for a variety of teaching tools, visit us at RHTeachersLibrarians.com

Library of Congress Cataloging-in-Publication Data is available upon request.
ISBN 978-0-593-38207-3 (trade pbk.) — ISBN 978-0-593-38208-0 (ebook)

The text of this book is set in 11.75-point Janson MT Pro.
Interior design by Andrea Lau

Printed in the United States of America
10 9 8 7 6 5 4 3 2 1
First Edition

To all the teens who didn't know they had a place in the world:

I see you. You belong.

Like a Love Song

Chapter 1

Everything's Wonderful

Nothing can prepare you for the bright lights of fame. *Nothing.* When I'm stepping onto a stage, the spotlight is a warm embrace. But when I'm walking a red carpet, the spotlight is cold, the camera's flashes little daggers of ice, making my heart speed up in turn.

I'm lucky I'm not alone tonight.

Trent is by my side as we pull up to the E! People's Choice Awards, but it takes him a moment to look away from the paparazzi's cameras and turn to me. He smiles, his Hollywood-white teeth bright. Deliberately, he puts his arm around me, and the butterflies in my stomach calm down. I feel elevated.

We're immediately guided from our limo by security people wearing black suits and earpieces. We barely have time to exchange another look before we're stepping onto the international symbol of fame and fortune: the red carpet.

"Natalie, when is your new album coming out?" asks one of the paparazzi.

"Natalie! Over here!" another shouts. "Are you excited about tonight? Do you think you'll win Female Artist of the Year?"

"Natalie!"

"Natalie, over here!"

"Natalie!"

The trick to posing on the red carpet is to suck in your breath, plaster on your most photogenic expression—for me, an open smile—and ignore everything the paparazzi say. Nobody looks good mid-speech, and this is all about looking good. Force your eyes to stay open, but somehow make it seem natural. You'll get used to the flashing lights eventually, seeing nothing but white and black dots in your vision. When that happens, only smile brighter.

One foot in front of the other. I can totally do this. Breathe in, breathe out.

I'm wearing a dress with an asymmetrical hem, shorter in the front and flowing down to the ground in the back, lilac tones deepening into purple. The torso is strapless and covered in what my stylist, Erin, assured me were tasteful sequins. The dress is sexy and beautiful, but it doesn't make me very comfortable—with a flat chest, I'm always worried a strapless dress is going to fall down. My heels are golden stilettos, and I'm glad that at least these aren't pointy. They're open sandals that show off my toes painted in lilac to match my skirt.

"Trent Nicholson! Trent!" another paparazzo shouts. "Are you upset you haven't been nominated this year? Do you think your last movie deserved it?"

Trent's grip on my waist tightens to the point of discomfort, but I'm too busy counting breaths in my head to look at him. Four seconds in, hold for seven, let go for eight.

Tonight is my night. I have to look . . . perfect.

I glance up at him and watch a frown pass over his face as he hurries forward, pulling me along with him. I hesitate, giving him a small confused smile. *What are you doing?* I try to telepathically communicate with my eyes. *This is the time for my solo shots. Go right along.*

Trent rolls his eyes and sighs, but eventually nods.

The Great American Sweethearts.

"Natalie, over here!"

The voices pull me back in, so I let myself drown in them. I turn sideways, showing off my bare back, tilting my head toward the cameras just enough that no belly rolls will show. I have rehearsed this a thousand times. Only turn twenty degrees. Never forty-five.

This is going to be okay. Gripping my Chanel purse close to my body, I repeat the mantra: *It's going to be okay.* I've worked all my life for tonight. And tonight is the night that I'll find out if it was all worth it. If I've succeeded or failed.

If I'm the Female Artist of the Year, or . . . a nominee.

Not Latin Artist of the Year. *Female Artist of the Year*, period.

A woman with her hair in a tight bun beckons me forward, and the next person, a hot star from a new HBO series, steps onto the red carpet. And like that, the paparazzi have a new focus.

I keep walking as they scream, "Savannah! Is it true that you're dating your costar? Savannah!" I'm still on the red carpet before the venue, but here the scene changes from paparazzi to mingling artists and TV cameras with red-carpet correspondents asking who you're wearing. My stomach turns as I scan the space for Trent.

Away from the flashing cameras, I feel a little safer, but I'm still clutching my purse for dear life. I need some reassurance, some positivity. I need to be told that I look great and that I will win tonight. I need to find my boyfriend.

Finally, I spot his blond, combed-back hair and his Armani suit. As I start toward him, the Ariana Grande song that's been blaring through the speakers fades out and my latest hit, "Together Forever," starts playing. My face lights up immediately. It's a remixed version by my good friend Padma—aka DJ Lotus—and hearing my lyrics blasted over the sound system eases my nerves. People like Trent will never understand what it's like to walk into a room full of people who are completely confident in their place in the world and feel like you don't belong. Knowing that they're all listening to my voice telling them that I *do* belong, as much as they do? That's power. And it's exhilarating in ways I can't even begin to describe.

I hold my head high as my voice on the track punctuates my steps. I want to get to Trent before the chorus, though he must have recognized my song already.

My steps slow when I see that he's talking to someone. Reese Brown, the newest Angel, a philanthropist who loves talking about natural beauty on her Instagram and has a huge following for posting no-makeup photos.

Of course, she has an objectively perfect face and has mastered the art of the selfie.

Trent touches her arm, and they laugh together.

Above us, the song reaches its chorus: *We'll be together forever, forever together.*

My nostrils flare in irritation. I kind of want to punch them both.

My carefully curated image is that I would *never* punch someone. But sometimes I feel things so strongly, it's difficult not to react. In elementary school, I got suspended because I grabbed a girl by her ponytail and swung her around. (She *had* been calling me names all day.) I remember being so angry, and then later, Mom being even angrier. I got an earful about Latinx stereotypes and how I had to fight against them. Be the Good Brazilian. Set the Example.

A lot of capitalized mottos that meant I had to control my emotions.

I was eight at the time, my first year in the United States. Now, nine years later, I channel that tight-fisted little girl as I scan the crowd.

I walk up to them with my brightest smile, interrupting their conversation. "Hi, everyone!" I grab Trent's arm, leaning toward him.

Okay. It's not my strongest opening line, but I'm nervous and the strap of my purse is starting to cut into my wrist.

I'm acutely aware of the way Reese is looking me up and down, and how she glances back up at Trent. "Hi, Natalie," she says slowly.

Trent puts an arm around my shoulders, but it feels awkward somehow. "What's up?"

What's up? I mouth at him, cocking an eyebrow. All that's missing is a *bro*.

"You know Reese, right?" He points at her, and then winks.

Together forever, forever together.

Four seconds of breathing in, hold for seven seconds, let go for eight.

I let go of his arm so I can hold my purse closer to my stomach.

"Not formally. Nice to meet you, Reese."

"Likewise," she says with a short ridiculous bow, and then chuckles.

Narrowing my eyes, I try to think of something clever to say, but right now I'm a little confused. I press my lips together, before my agent Bobbi's voice in my head tells me that it'll ruin my lipstick, so I muster all the patience I have, nod to them both, and then turn away.

He's going to come after me.

Because tonight is my night. He knows how hard I've worked for tonight.

Except, after walking for several seconds, clutching my purse so tightly my knuckles are turning from brown to white, Trent doesn't call out my name or turn me around in a romantic gesture. He doesn't grab my waist or—

Someone bumps into me, and it's not Trent.

The impact knocks the purse out of my hands, and all its contents spill on the carpet.

"Oh God, I'm so sorry, I was looking at a meme—" he says, the British accent catching me off guard.

I still choose to ignore him as he kneels down to gather my things. This is so embarrassing. "It's okay," I tell him, my tone sharper than usual. But I need my purse, I need my . . .

He takes my inhaler. Not my phone, my keys, my lipstick, or even my little notepad for impromptu lyric writing. He goes for the little inhaler.

My horror doesn't last too long, because when he gives

it to me, our hands touch, and I finally look at him. He has scruffy brown curls and a Victorian nose. He's white, but not Trent's tanned California-white. He's just . . . very white. His cheeks are pink, like he's flustered, and his eyes are a deep green, with long dark eyelashes.

He smiles hesitantly. And when I snatch the inhaler from his hands, my eyes wide, saying, "This is for somebody else," he offers me a lopsided grin. I stick it in my purse as fast as I can, looking over my shoulder, but we're far enough away from the spotlight of the red carpet that nobody seems to care about us.

"Okay. Um, here, your phone," he says.

I take my phone, but the screen is lit up with notifications, and I realize I forgot to set it to Do Not Disturb mode. My battery's probably going to die soon. I sigh.

"Are you okay? Your hands are shaking," he says, his British accent thick.

I shove the phone into my purse, along with keys, lipstick, and notebook, and stand up so fast that I get dizzy. "Yes, I'm okay," I respond, annoyed and embarrassed and, *God,* I just want this to be over.

He stands up as well. It looks like his suit doesn't fit him right. It's navy blue, but I don't recognize the cut. I can tell it's not Armani. He must notice me staring, because his grin goes lopsided again, and he says, "It's my first time at this, too. But don't be nervous. It's a stupid facade anyway."

I part my lips, blinking slowly.

"Wh—?"

He shrugs. "It's so frivolous, just shallow people making believe." He pauses, his mouth tugging down at the corners. "I wish I weren't here as well. I bet you can think of a thousand better ways to spend your Friday evening, right?" He chuckles and pats my arm in a friendly manner. "It'll be over before you know it."

"Stupid?" I say, taking a step back. The culmination of everything I've worked for my entire career? *Stupid?* Who does this guy think he is? Does he think he's *better* than—?

Either ignoring my expression or unbothered by my deep offense, he offers his hand. "I'm William Ainsley, by the way."

For a second, I consider introducing myself as *frivolous and shallow*, but instead I stare at his hand, shake my head, and walk away, purse clutched to my stomach.

I take another breath and refocus on my wonderful evening. My night to shine.

Chapter 2

This Is Important, Babe

*T*he awards ceremony is held at Barker Hangar in Santa Monica again this year, and though I was here two years ago presenting a minor award, now I have my own dressing room backstage. I can't help but feel like I've finally made it.

Bobbi comes by every few minutes with the latest gossip, and Trent sits on the couch, scrolling through his phone, not really here—like his phone is more important—and, honestly, that's okay for now. I can't focus on him while preparing for my big night. I'm sitting in front of the mirror, practicing for the award I'm presenting before my own category, when Bobbi once again swoops into the dressing room.

Bobbi is the fairy godmother of agents, with good humor and endless patience for my mom's incessant questions from day one. She's a middle-aged Black woman with a kid of her own who's in college in Chicago. She's also got the most amazing collection of suits.

Case in point: Today, she's in a dark-purple satin pantsuit with a black button-down underneath.

Bobbi scans my face and asks, "Anything wrong?"

"No, I—"

She spreads her arms wide. "Yes! Who's the most glorious, the most beautiful, the greatest to ever exist?"

I turn to her with a coy smile. "I am?"

Bobbi closes the door behind her. "Who's going to receive her first Female Artist of the Year award from these suckers and make sure they love you more each second?"

My chest flutters. I get up, standing five inches taller. "I am!"

Bobbi's grinning from ear to ear. She pulls me into a hug, careful not to mess up my straightened hair, which reaches my waistline. "And why is that?"

I hug her back, beaming. "Because I'm *good*."

"That's the spirit, Natalie." She kisses my cheek on instinct, then pulls back with wide eyes. I turn to the mirror immediately, but upon inspection, her matte lipstick didn't leave a mark. "Let's go backstage so you can give someone else their award, and then you come back to rest for a sweet second before you're crowned queen of the night."

Now, that's something I wouldn't mind putting in my Instagram bio. Queen.

I bite the insides of my cheeks in anticipation. Turning around to check on Trent, I see that he's still slouched on the velvet couch. Every time I meet his eye, he seems to look away. He hasn't even told me good luck yet.

But I'm not going to beg for attention. If he's busy, then so be it.

I head toward the stage.

A PA in a black suit hands me the envelope and winks at me. Her friendly gesture feels like more encouragement than my boyfriend's given me today.

The first time you step on a stage, it's a glorious moment.

The five hundredth time, it's just as magical.

It's not the same as selling out an arena with the audience scream-singing the lyrics you wrote in your bedroom late at night, but it's still incredible.

Everyone cheers as I cross the stage. My calves are already aching, but I push through with my most gorgeous smile, holding the little orange envelope in my hands.

Under the hot, bright lights, I play my part. Create a little suspense, even though I'm trying to find Mom in the rows of VIP spectators. I read from the teleprompter, then open the envelope, biting my lip, and call out the winner for TV Drama of the Year. The cast, writers, and producers explode with excitement, and I clap enthusiastically for a show I've never watched. As they come onstage, I gracefully step aside and let them have their moment.

Then I hug them, all these people I've never met, like we're longtime friends, like everyone here is pals. One of the women links an arm through mine while a writer squeezes in his two cents before the music starts playing him off. I lean into her like she's my favorite person in the world, but I don't even know her name.

The front row, before the VIP section of the crowd starts, is actually reserved for the cameras. A beehive of photographers take a thousand pictures without drawing any attention to themselves, while suspended cameras film the event. We all know not to glance at the cameras. We all know we're just posing.

When the lights go down and a new musical number signals the commercial break between awards, Bobbi comes to take me back to my dressing room, and I realize I don't feel so magical anymore. Exhausted, maybe.

Bobbi links her arm with mine. "Wasn't that wonderful?"

"Yes, it was," I reply without thinking, feigning enthusiasm I'm not feeling.

Weird.

She stops me before we reach my dressing room and takes my hands. "Five minutes, okay? You have five minutes to go over your thank-you speech, and then, if—I mean *when* you win, Gemma Santiago is 'surprising' you by coming backstage to get you—"

I start. "Gemma Santiago? She's giving the award?" Bobbi nods, and there's a spark of joy in me that I can't control. "Are you kidding me? I've sung her songs in the shower all my life. I've always wanted to— I've never met her. I really wanted to, but . . . but it never happened. *She's* the one—?"

"Be in your dressing room, doing something cute," Bobbi advises. She's about to turn and go but she stops herself. "And tell Trent to get lost. He shouldn't be there if they come for you. This moment is yours."

I nod.

But I remain standing, feeling a little off.

While the commercial break music reverberates backstage, my mind swirls: my boyfriend, talking to the hottest new Angel; my inhaler in the purse that's in my dressing room. Frivolous, superficial. *Gemma Santiago?*

My stomach churns.

Trent appears in the corridor and starts my way.

"Natalie. Whoa. I had forgotten how hot you look tonight."

I give him a small smile. Everything's going to be fine. I'm probably just nervous.

"Thanks. You look good, too. Who are you wearing?" I ask, widening my eyes as though I'm interviewing him on the red carpet, and he gives me an awkward laugh.

"Yeah." He nods for a moment, then, as if he's remembered it now, says, "Listen, can we talk real quick?"

His slight frown, the way his hands are tucked into the pockets of his pants . . . I step closer, put my hands on his chest, and tease, "Oh, you look so serious like that. Are you going to propose or something? I'm going to have to politely decline. I'm only seventeen. Maybe in a few years, same place?"

Trent lets out a strangled laugh. He puts his hands on mine. "You're funny."

"I'm delightful," I reply.

"You are. Which is why this is so hard."

"What—?"

Trent takes my hands from his chest and holds them. I vaguely notice some light around us, but I'm too shocked to look away.

"I met someone else. You remember Reese, right? We've been DMing for a while now, and I think she's the real thing."

Reese.

My jaw drops. I hear someone call my name, but I just put my hand up. The eight-year-old in me is ready to fight. What I want, like I've never wanted anything, is to punch Trent in his perfect face.

"This is important, babe," he says, his frown deepening. "I'm telling you I think I've fallen in love. Aren't you supposed to be happy for me?"

I can't take it. I can't.

"You said you loved *me*, you asshole!" I yell in his face, my hand hitting his chest. He takes a step back.

"Well, I did! But things change," he answers, all the while sounding like the nice guy everyone thinks he is. A perfect gentleman.

A perfect jerk.

"These past eight months have been really good," he continues with a stupid fake smile. "We've been through a lot. Nominated best couple on Instagram and trended how many times?" Trent puts a hand on my arm, and I yank it back. "I've lost count!"

"This isn't happening." I say and shut my eyes.

If I can't see him, he can't see me. This is not happening. None of this is. If I keep my eyes screwed shut for long enough, I know I can be back in my living room under a blanket with a canja bowl on my lap and Mom by my side.

"I didn't even want to come here today," he laments. "It's your award. I respect that. But why should I have to come to events that don't involve me in any way, just because of you? Reese would never ask that of me."

I get on my tiptoes, so I'm right in his face, speaking between gritted teeth. "Did you wait until *my* moment to make *me* feel like trash before I'm told I'm a queen? Screw you, Nicholson!"

My voice is high-pitched and breaking.

I feel the tears coming, and I can't stop the words pouring out of my mouth.

"You're supposed to be a supportive boyfriend who is not breaking up with me minutes before my award, you self-centered, egocentric son of a—"

"Honey!" Bobbi yells, exasperated but firm.

I take a step back.

Oh.

My.

God.

The camera crew is here. Gemma Santiago, a Latina queen who's made history for the past decade, is here. With her vibrant golden dress, her signature full red lips, and the most awkward expression I've ever seen.

She's still holding the envelope, the one that probably has my name in it.

It's golden, too.

Bobbi looks like she's arrived in a rush. Everyone seems flustered. The camera operator mouths an apology, but they don't stop streaming.

"Oh no," I murmur, but the tears are coming, and I can't stop them. "Oh no."

It's the moment I've been dreaming of. And it's a complete mess.

Bobbi turns to the camera operator again. "Can't you stop filming?!"

He shakes his head. "It's live."

Trent smiles at the camera and waves. I feel my makeup melting from sweat and tears.

Bobbi comes into the frame, and as she puts an arm protectively around me, she whispers in my ear, "I told you to be in your dressing room. They were coming to get you. Didn't you realize the commercial break was over?"

I feel the warm tears rolling down my cheeks. Yes, that's definitely going to leave a trail. I wipe them away with the back of my hands, ignoring Bobbi and Trent, who's still next to me.

I square my shoulders and turn to the camera, stepping in front of my ex-boyfriend.

"Okay, let's do this."

Chapter 3

Girl, Memefied

y friends will be here any minute, but while I wait, it's just me and the internet.

At least my dream mentor, Gemma Santiago, hasn't tweeted about me or reposted one of the memes, because it feels like, in this past week, everyone else has.

I've buried myself under a fortress of duvets. Mom would hate to see that the AC is on during an early-September California day—even when California is cold, it isn't exactly *cold*—but I'm purposely making my room ridiculously icy. This is the life I'm choosing to live right now, under the covers.

I was watching the fourth season of *Make Me a Royal*, but now it's background noise. Gretta, the commoner who's in love with the prince, is about to make him lose his crown for the sake of their love. "Losers!" I yell at the TV. I use my phone to pause the show.

And, for the millionth time this morning, I open Instagram and click the tagged pictures.

A screen-size me is yelling in a loop: "Did you wait until *my* moment to make *me* feel like trash before I'm told I'm a queen?"

Again and again and again.

I sigh and start scrolling. So many memes with that scene alone.

One caption is ME WHEN MOM SAYS I CAN'T GO TO A BTS CONCERT. Another caption reads, ME WHEN A PROFESSOR DOESN'T GIVE ME AN A.

I scroll down fast until the thumbnail changes. I pause and let it play. It's me staring at the camera with wide eyes and melted dark makeup. "Oh no," I say in the video, and then it becomes a remix of me saying it over and over and over again. Most of the videos are imported from TikTok. The one time I opened TikTok, I saw people acting out the scene with my music playing, people dancing to my speech, and it . . . wasn't great.

"Ugh," I groan, shoving my phone into the blanket as if, just like that, everything will go away.

Mom barges in without knocking. She starts with "Your friends—" but stops, frowns, looks up at the AC disapprovingly, then apparently chooses her battle and walks to the bed. "Nati, filha."

"Natalie," I correct her.

A knee-jerk reaction that shouldn't have happened, because now all sympathy is gone from her round hazel eyes, and she's glaring at me. "Your name is Natalia," she says, with a strong Brazilian accent. "Na-ta-li-a," she repeats. "And Nati is a loving nickname. Everyone named Natalia has that nickname."

Everyone Brazilian, living in Brazil. But I don't say that.

"Natalie's a stage name," I offer. One that I insist all my friends call me, too.

Mom seems to accept that for now. She lies down and gestures for me to do the same. I resist for about a millisecond before I give up on seeming tough, and lie down as well, letting Mom cuddle me. Back when we lived in Brazil in Grandma's house, we shared a room and used to cuddle every night. She would kiss my head, and we would talk quietly about how our day had been. Usually, it was my favorite time of the day.

When Mom worked on the remodel of the National Library in Rio de Janeiro, she created a futuristic design inspired by Oscar Niemeyer that attracted attention from international architecture firms. I was eight at the time. She was offered jobs in Los Angeles, Boston, Singapore, and Milan. Even though she didn't speak fluent English at the time, she signed with the firm in Los Angeles. The one with the best career plan and highest salary.

Which also turned out to be the hub of the entertainment industry.

With the security of Mom's new job came mine. I was scouted in a talent show at my arts school in LA, and then I signed with Bobbi, the best agent ever, who brought in a wonderful marketing and PR team. Now I have a gold and a platinum album and two world tours behind me.

And the internet doesn't care about any of that, because I'm the new hottest meme.

"You have to forget that night," Mom murmurs, holding me close. I let her hold me and sigh softly. For a second I'm surprised she's read my mind, then I realize my silence is probably pretty obvious. "For a little bit, if anything."

Just above a whisper, I confess, "I'm afraid, Mami . . ."

She doesn't ask why. With her mom powers, she knows. "They'll forget about it eventually. You've earned their respect."

I close my eyes and allow myself to feel safe, even if I don't believe her.

"I came in to say your friends texted me that they'll be a little late because they stopped at a bakery." She pauses. "Maybe that part was a surprise, actually. Anyway, they texted me because they said your phone was probably turned off. Is it?"

I don't respond.

She sighs and kisses the top of my head, just like when I was a little kid.

Padma—DJ Lotus—and Brenda enter my room without any knocking, either, because no one respects my privacy, be it Mom or my friends. But Brenda is bringing sprinkled doughnuts, my favorite, and Padma is carrying a bag of chips, so I don't comment on that.

"I love sprinkles," I murmur, sitting up.

Padma is the coolest person I've met since becoming famous. Brenda is my only non-famous friend who stayed in my tiny circle because she loved me and not because she wanted things. Along the way, they became girlfriends. They're super cute together. Even though I feel down about this whole Trent mess, it makes me happy to see them so happy.

"Girl, you love *us*. You don't get to say you love sprinkles before you say you love us," Padma says with a frown as she sits by my side.

Brenda nods, but shoves the box of doughnuts my way, anyway. "OMG, is this *Make Me a Royal*? I haven't watched the new season yet. Are Gretta and Timothy together?" She grabs my phone to unpause it.

I yank it back from her hands and force-close Netflix. "Gretta and Timothy are losers," I say. She glares at me, and Padma chuckles, getting under the blanket with me.

"It's Antarctica in here. Where are the penguins?" Padma scrunches her nose.

Brenda reluctantly gets under the blankets on my other side. She opens the doughnut box and unceremoniously grabs herself one.

"Making fun of me on the internet." I shrug.

They exchange a look. I roll my eyes and rest my head on Padma's shoulder. She has a pixie cut, so her hair doesn't bother me when I want to cuddle—Brenda's long, light hair always ends up getting in my mouth, even when we hug.

Brenda is the only other Brazilian I know in the States. We met in school my first year here, when I was eight and she was nine, and though her family's originally from Recife and mine from São Paulo, it was easy to bond over the fact that no American can properly pronounce Recife *or* São Paulo.

I met Padma way later, only last year, before I went on my most recent world tour. My publicist connected us to make some music, and we ended up talking in the studio for hours about growing up with reruns of children shows from a decade ago: mine from Brazil, hers from Pakistan. It made our vocabulary in our native tongues a little limited now that we're teenagers. I can't speak about politics or global warming in Portuguese, but you'd be surprised how many ways I can say that the kitten is fluffy and sweet.

Padma leans back and makes a funny face. "Your hair smells *bad*, Natalie."

I take a doughnut from the box on Brenda's lap. "Thanks, friend. You're so supportive."

"Padma has a point, though," Brenda tells me. "I know what happened was horrible. We brought comfort food. We love you. We hate Trent. But you have to get back to your routine. And do things like, uh, shower." She makes a face.

Padma runs her hands through her short hair. Her dark brown fingers shimmer with several silver rings, and it looks beyond cool. If I tried that, I'd probably seem like I was trying too hard. Everything with her is effortless. It makes me want to hug her even as she's talking. "Okay, spill. How are you feeling?"

"I just hate everything right now," I say. "There are memes of *everything*. My face is everywhere. I thought I could write my suffering into a song, but apparently I can't—" I gesture to my writing pad on the side table. Its blank pages mock me.

"Did you uninstall Twitter and Insta like you promised Bobbi?" Brenda asks, and before I can respond, she grabs my phone. She knows the password—Mom's birthdate—and when she unlocks it, she groans and shows the screen to Padma.

Padma snorts. "You're using the web version of Instagram? You have got to stop." She takes the bag of chips and shoves it in my general direction.

I take the bag and cram chips in my mouth. "It's so humiliating," I say around a mouthful. Brenda shakes her head, probably closing the tabs. "And Trent hasn't called."

"Of course he hasn't called. He's a dick," Brenda says, more to herself than me, based on how her eyes are still on my phone. "You can't expect him to call. He won't."

I look down. "But I miss him."

Padma touches my shoulder. "Do you, though?"

Before I can answer, Brenda sighs heavily, hugging me close, a proper hug this time. "You know what we're going to do? We're going to watch that old show your mom is obsessed with, and we're going to sleep over. It's going to heal everything."

Padma hugs my other side. I close my eyes and offer a little smile. "Yes!" She kisses my cheek.

Brenda adds, "And then you're going to call Bobbi back, because she's *this* close to breaking into my AP physics class to ask about you."

I laugh. "Bobbi wants me to make some kind of triumphant comeback. But I'm not feeling it. My PR team is gonna stare at me like I'm a mess that can't be fixed."

They pull away. Padma holds me by the shoulders and looks deep into my eyes, which are probably red from crying. "You don't need any fixing, you hear me, Natalie? That's not it. You were in a difficult position. So what? It happens! All of our heroes have been in some sort of scandal. This is the first time where people have seen you're *real* and you get pissed off. Before, all they saw was perfect little Miss America. You've given them realness."

I touch her hands on my shoulders and pull them back. "I've given them GIF content for days."

"Why can't it be both?" Brenda chirps.

Padma touches my arm to bring my attention back to her.

"It happens. And it happened. And that's okay. What has Auntie said about that?"

"Mom?" I frown, then take the deepest breath I've taken all day. "Well, she thinks I should be in Brazil for a while. Hang out with my family, stay away from LA and the cameras. Until it all blows over."

Brenda groans. "Can you take me with you? Mom wants me to think about colleges and, um, no thanks! I don't even know where I can get in with my *meh* GPA."

"You two are in serious need of pep talks, gotta say." Padma shakes her head. "Why aren't you already there? You know we're both here for you, but if you can stay with your grandparents and a bunch of cousins, isn't that even better?"

I sink in the bed and bring my comforter up to my chin.

Not really, I think to myself. I'm not that confident in my Portuguese. So I can't communicate with my grandparents, because they don't speak good English, and while some of my cousins do, they all just . . . they just give me these judgmental looks. So I'm not going back unless someone shoves me into an airplane.

But instead I say, "Aaaaaanyway."

Padma urges Brenda to give her my phone. She also knows the password. "What's the name of that soap opera? The one with the feminist lawyer who wants to start a revolution and falls in love with a prince?"

Cordel Encantado is a good show.

Brenda gets on her knees and says, "Ooh, what if we watched *Girl, Interrupted*? Angelina Jolie is my dream in that movie."

"Don't." Padma raises a finger. "She's old enough to be your mother. Please."

"You're just jealous," Brenda teases, cocking an eyebrow.

And then she bridges the distance, literally stepping on me to get to Padma and give her girlfriend a peck. I roll my eyes, but I'm used to third-wheeling.

Brenda snuggles in between us, grabs another doughnut, then surveys me with a smirk. "What about *Girl, Memefied*?"

I let out an inhuman noise of annoyance, but we all laugh at that.

✦

I jolt awake from a nightmare in which I'm dancing around in Carmen Miranda's clothing at a big awards show and everyone tells me to go back to Brazil. I wake up feeling sweaty and nauseous, with Brenda's legs thrown over me and Padma's face buried in my neck. I not-so-gently push them aside, take my phone, and go to my en suite bathroom.

The cold water on my face clears away the weird nightmare feeling, but I'm still more asleep than awake when I sit to pee. As per usual, I grab my phone to scroll through social media, but my apps are all gone.

Stubbornly, I access Twitter from the phone browser.

It's supposed to be a quick thing. Just check what everyone's up to—what I've been missing this week.

It's not a quick thing.

The first thing I see upon logging in? A fan account posting a picture of Trent and Reese. They're holding hands and looking passionately into each other's eyes. The caption is only a bunch of heart-eyes emojis.

I feel like I'm going to be sick.

I can't believe they're already *dating*. Posing together like some kind of *power couple*. I mean, it's only been a week since he dumped me!

I go to Trent's Twitter account to see what he's been tweeting and release a breath of relief. He's posted pictures of himself, broody and handsome in Hugo Boss this week, and—is that my favorite Thai restaurant? Possibly. I can't tell. But at least he's not posting pictures with *her* . . . yet.

I grit my teeth and flush. With my pants still down and my eyes still glued to the phone screen, I click his likes.

The first one is of me.

Or, well, a version of me.

In the tweet I've got my index finger pressed to his chest. The caption is YOU PROMISED YOU'D MAKE ME QUEEN. There are thousands of likes and retweets.

And Trent Nicholson, the boy I dated for the past eight months, liked it.

"Escroto," I curse, but I sort of want to cry, too.

With a lot more strength than necessary, I poke my phone to close the app. The phone goes flying out of my hand . . .

. . . and splashes into the toilet. I yelp, take a step back, and nearly trip on the pool of my pants around my ankles.

For a moment, I just stand there, dazed. This is about as far away from being a queen as I could get.

Then I pull up my pants and sigh. Someone has to fish that phone out of the toilet.

And someone's got to do something about the pathetic mess I've become.

Chapter 4

There's the Easy Way Out, and There's Brazil

either Padma nor Brenda appreciates it when I pull my bedroom curtains open, letting an aggressive amount of sunlight into the once-dark room. Both of them groan, and Padma screams that she hates me, but I don't really mind. After this morning's unexpected ritual of washing my hands a thousand times, I'm on a mission.

I jump on the end of the bed, and yank the blanket away from Brenda when she tries to cover her head with it.

"Focus, girls! I need you alert."

Padma starts talking in Sindhi, and I can't tell if she's cursing at me or just cursing me. Brenda eventually sits up, half zombie, half gas-station doll forgotten by time.

"I don't want to be awake right now. I don't want to—can I not be awake right now?"

"No, Brenda, you have to be awake. I need to talk to you." I play-slap her arm.

"Ouch! I'm awake! I'm awake!"

"Good. You have Bobbi's phone number, right? Where's your phone? I need to call her."

"I can't believe you woke us up for this. What time—?" Padma grabs her own phone from under the pillow. "It's eight in the morning! I'm a DJ, I'm like a bat! I thrive in darkness!" Unceremoniously, she flops back on the bed and covers her head with the blanket.

"Just—" Brenda gestures dismissively and yawns. "Just call her using your phone, Jesus."

"I . . . There was an incident with my phone." I press my lips together in a thin line.

Brenda's too sleepy to catch my distress.

"Brenda!" I yell. Padma tries to kick me from under the blanket, but I'm much too skillful to be hit by a sleeping zombie. "Where's your phone?"

She rolls her eyes and points at the bag she dropped by the door last night when she arrived.

Perfect.

I jump out of the bed, and the second I leave, Brenda crawls back under the blanket to snuggle up to her girl-friend. I'm betting in a half second she'll be back asleep.

I rifle through Brenda's curiously numerous hoodies until I find her phone. I'm a little breathless when I finally find Bobbi's contact—listed under *"Natalie's Agent-Mom."*

Bobbi answers on the second ring.

"Hello, Brenda?"

"It's me, Bobbi. Natalie," I tell her. "Gather the team. We need to do something about this shit."

Bobbi lets out a joyful whoop, and then says, "Don't you swear, Natalie. Language. But yes. Meet me at my office in an hour."

The large office feels almost like a second home to me. It gives me a sense of comfort as I walk in, even though I'm being ushered into a meeting room where Ashley is sitting cross-legged on the couch opposite Bobbi. The director of the PR and marketing team is a woman in her forties with a sleek bob and red lipstick, which is always absolutely impeccable. She's a lot more serious than any other adult I work with, and I find her intimidating, but Ashley has warranted my trust and eternal gratitude for introducing me to Padma.

"Hi, so good to see you, Ashley!" I offer her my hand. "Sorry this is such short notice."

Bobbi appears behind me a second later. "It's true. Thank you for coming so quickly, Ashley." She puts a hand on my shoulder with a motherly smile.

"Of course." Ashley stands to shake my hand and then sits down again. She has her assistant with her, a man in his twenties who is so cute that I'm suddenly ashamed of my only-slightly-better-than-pajamas yoga pants and oversize hoodie.

I pretend I'm scratching my nose with my shoulder to try and catch a whiff of the smell. Not great.

"Merda," I curse.

Ashley glances at me curiously, but Bobbi knows what it means and gives me a meaningful glare.

"Okay, let's start." Ashley clears her throat and gestures for us to begin.

Bobbi turns to me. "Natalie contacted me earlier today. She's interested in reconstructing her image after the People's Choice Awards incident."

They both stare at me, like they expect some big revelation.

I haven't washed my hair in almost a week, have barely showered, and even dropped my phone in the toilet this morning. I don't know what they expect from *me*. So I nod in agreement.

"Well," Ashley says, once it's clear they're not getting anything else. She pushes her glasses up the bridge of her nose. "No drugs, no violence, no sex workers. This shouldn't be too hard to deal with."

I open and close my mouth, shooting a quick look at Bobbi. She seems unfazed.

"The bar isn't very high, is it?" I frown. "I mean, I'm

seventeen. Most of those things sound . . . not very possible for someone my age to be involved in—"

Ashley doesn't blink. "You'd be surprised."

"Okay, so it's not quite that scandalous, it's just . . ." I sigh, gazing at my sneakers. "It's bad. Everyone's making jokes online and they're *tagging* me in all of that. They want me to see that they think I'm a joke."

"Don't be discouraged," Ashley says. "There are no lawsuits working against us and no inappropriate pictures leaked. I can assure you that getting the public to respect you again is going to be a piece of cake."

Right now, it doesn't feel like a piece of cake.

Ashley turns to her assistant. "Christopher, are you taking notes?" He shows her his notebook, and she hums in acknowledgment before turning back to us. "Perfect. Is there anything at all we should know before developing your comeback strategy?"

"Um. I dropped my phone in the toilet this morning?" I offer.

Christopher looks confused, his pen hovering over the pad.

Bobbi clears her throat and pulls a few locs behind her shoulder. "I'll ask my assistant to get you a new one. I think Ashley meant anything as in, have you contacted Trent? Has he contacted you? Does he have sensitive pictures or videos of you?"

I cringe. "Ew, no, no, and no. He's dead to me."

Which isn't entirely true. But it feels way more dignified than saying that what really broke my heart and my phone was seeing him laughing at my expense along with the rest of the internet.

"Brilliant." Ashley turns to Bobbi. "How are the charts?"

"Dipping, I'm afraid." Bobbi passes her a closed folder. As Ashley starts going over some papers, Bobbi adds, "No longer number one. We lost ground this week, but I still think we can make a solid comeback if we focus on her image. She doesn't need to release any new music so soon. She's just got out of a world tour."

"Of course. That wouldn't be necessary." Ashley closes the folder and hands it to Christopher, who reviews its contents. No one offers a folder to me. I'm about to ask whether my numbers are *that* bad when Ashley turns back to me with a crimson smile. "There are two ways we can do this, Natalie. You can give them something else to talk about, or we can build on your good-girl image. Send you to a third-world country so you can do some community work. People love charity."

I sit up. My voice rising, I tell her, "Don't say *third-world* country. It's extremely elitist, and honestly, you're putting yourself, as an American, above folks that have been colonized."

By my side, I hear Bobbi whisper, "Brazilian."

Ashley cocks an eyebrow. "I'm sorry, Natalie. I didn't

realize you were so political. If that's your inclination, we can find a way for you to spend some time in Brazil, making sure you're filmed and photographed there so your audience knows you care."

"I— That's not—that's not what I said." I feel my face flush.

We're in a staring contest, Ashley and I, and the worst part is that I can tell she genuinely doesn't mean any harm by what she's saying. How do I tell her that I can be both outraged at her imperialist language and *also* not want to go back to my home country to do volunteer work with strangers instead of writing my music and living my life?

If I say that now, I'll sound like an entitled jerk.

Bobbi breaks the awkward silence, clearing her throat in a way that makes us both look at her, and shakes her head. "No, that won't do. I see your angle, but maybe keeping Natalie away from the spotlight while Trent is parading around with his new girlfriend would be detrimental to her image."

"Quite the contrary, actually," Ashley says. "Research shows that in situations like these, when the dumpee channels their humiliation into charitable acts, the public admires them and vilifies the person who left."

There. Are. So. Many. Words. About. This. That. I. Hate.

From Bobbi calling Reese *his new girlfriend* to my receiving the title of *dumpee,* I am not loving the way this meeting is going.

"All right, so what's the other option? The one about giving them something else to talk about?" I ask.

"Oh, of course. Your fan base is invested in your personal life. All we have to do is shake it up a little bit, as they say." She does a horrifying shoulder shimmy that I assume represents shaking things up. I catch her assistant's eyes, and we're both scarred for life. Ashley leans forward in earnest. "All you need is a new boyfriend."

Chapter 5

Who's with Me
to Start #NataQueen?

I wait for Ashley to start laughing. She doesn't.

Christopher has his head down again, taking notes. I sort of expected him to silently agree with me that this is *weird*.

Bobbi doesn't say anything, either.

I stare at both women, my jaw hanging open.

"You can't—you can't expect me to get a rebound this quickly! How would I even go out and meet people? I'll seem desperate! I already seem desperate enough, I just— I can't do this. This is— No!"

Ashley seems confused; Bobbi actually chuckles.

Like this is funny.

This is not funny. I'm seriously about to question their credentials. I can't be trusted to pee with my phone in my hands. How am I supposed to find someone to date?

"She doesn't mean for real," Bobbi says.

I narrow my eyes.

"Yes, obviously." Ashley nods. "I'm talking about a fake relationship. We do it all the time to promote movies, TV shows, and so forth. Stir up a little drama to create media interest, making sales higher. This is a fairly common practice. We already have a standard 'relationship' nondisclosure agreement, and I have contacts I can pass on to Bobbi to choose from, so you can be sure it's a suitable candidate. One who'll benefit from the public exposure as much as you."

Instead of being able to properly express how *not down* for this I am, all I can squeak out is a strangled little "That can't be legal."

Bobbi nods. "It is entirely legal. Another client I have—you'll understand that I won't disclose who—has recently gotten in a new relationship, but because he's in a boy band and fans tend not to respect their privacy, he's hired a team to shield the woman from the fans and spread rumors that he's with numerous other ladies, so they won't know what's true."

"That's not—that's not really the same," I try.

But my protest is obviously in vain. They have both already made up their mind about how super totally normal and cool this is.

Ashley explains, "This is a very old trick, Natalie. Earlier this week I staged paparazzi catching a 'couple' stealing kisses outside a movie set. They don't know each other that well, but they're costars in the movie, so it's excellent promo."

I sigh. "Yeah, okay, but I just can't do that."

This time, the silence is like a bomb I couldn't defuse in time. It blows up everyone's expectations of me and my triumphant comeback.

They all want to see me shine—well, Christopher's investment in my career is a little doubtful—and they probably think I'm being difficult. I hate the idea of pretending to like someone I don't. I've had to pretend so much already. Pretend that my skin is hairless and smooth, that my hair is straight like an arrow. I've even lost parts of myself to keep pretending, like losing every hint of my accent in vocal practice. If I pretend to be in *love* with someone I don't even know, won't that be even worse?

I clear my throat awkwardly and get up. "I'm so sorry to waste everyone's time. I'll keep thinking of other strategies, okay?"

Although she still seems a little upset, Ashley gamely says, "We can rebuild your image in smaller ways. I'll have my team work on a plan and send it to Bobbi as soon as possible. It just might take a little longer for the effects to show."

I nod.

Bobbi stands as well and tells me, "Wait in the other room, all right? I have some things to discuss with Ashley, and you can have my assistant get you a new phone."

I nod again. "I'm sorry."

"Don't be silly," Bobbi says, and she kisses the top of my head.

It feels like I've let everyone down. Defeated, I force a smile, waving to Ashley and Christopher before I go, and leave the adults to it.

I'm a mess of nervous energy and fear that I've blown my one chance at a comeback when I stop at Linda's desk on my way out.

Bobbi's assistant is a white woman in her early thirties, with a face covered in freckles and a nineties sense of fashion. Linda is always nice to me in an impersonal kind of way that makes me think she's not into pop music or celebrities, which has always made me wonder about her career choices.

The second I ask her for a new phone, she tells me to please wait a second, then calls an intern to go buy me one. Just like that.

"It'll be here in a second," she says, her attention returning to her computer.

It's not here in a second.

My leg starts going up and down, and I look around for something to do, but everyone's busy and I don't want to interrupt them.

I stare down at the floor.

Maybe I should work, too?

"Excuse me, Linda? I'm sorry to bother," I say, getting up from the black velvet couch. "But do you have a piece of paper or something? And a pen. Or pencil. Or something."

She hands me a blank notepad and a pen that looks expensive. "Here you go."

"Thanks," I murmur, leafing through the pages as if there were a story they could tell.

They can't. But maybe I can.

I sit cross-legged on the couch again and pull my hood up, so I can pretend to be invisible. I think back on the memes comparing me to telenovela stars in overdramatic crying scenes, mixing up my name with typical Mexican names. What's a word that rhymes with xenophobia?

Frowning, I let the pen flow in tiny circles at the margin.

I think of the pictures of me crying, and the humiliation I felt, with the caption SOMEONE'S JUST BROKEN A NAIL.

I write:

Do they hate me because I'm a girl?
Do they hate me because I'm seventeen?
Do they hate me because I'm Brazilian?

I tap the paper with my pen. My words aren't lyrics yet but merely ideas. And do I really want to write about any of this? Do I really want to make this even more of a big deal than it is?

I cross out all three sentences.

"Hm."

Closing my eyes, I rest my head against the back of the couch until I'm facing the ceiling. I open my eyes and stare at the white. Write about what's on your heart, Natalia.

But maybe don't go too far.

. . . Do I miss Trent?

I suppose I miss Trent. I suppose anyone would. Doesn't everyone love him?

I flip to a clean page and keep trying to write lyrics, but none of my thoughts are poetic or linear. I end up drawing stick figures that can't sing.

When the intern comes back, I have no idea whether it's been five minutes or fifty. He hands the sealed box to Linda instead of me and is out of the room before I can thank him. Linda gives me her signature impersonal smile when she hands me the box, and then her phone rings, and I don't think she even hears my thank-yous.

In a few minutes, I have my new phone working again. The phone updates my apps, including Instagram and Twitter. I stop Twitter in time—I'm definitely not ready to go back to cyber-stalking Trent—but it's too late for Instagram, and my notifications start appearing.

I have another app that works with Instagram and only sends me notifications of people who have been verified by the app, so I'm not drowning in fan accounts and end up missing it when someone industry-important follows me or comments on one of my posts.

That's how I know that William Ainsley followed me on Instagram.

As in, the boy from the awards ceremony, who told me it was all stupid.

Who would have thought he'd be verified?

It makes me pause. I ignore the other notifications from pseudo-friends *wishing me well* and *oh my God you must be devastated,* and click on his account.

His profile picture is what can only be described as his attempt to become a tree, with several animals climbing their way up. Only the several animals are children. And he seems to be trying his best to accommodate them all on his arms and legs.

I count five children.

I frown. Is he a teen dad or something?

His bio reads: *Londoner. Actor. Sock enthusiast.*

My frown deepens.

His profile doesn't look very much like that of an actor, or even what I would imagine of a regular Londoner, though admittedly I don't know many Brits. It's not very . . . *fancy.* It's mostly pictures of him with an unholy number of kids, a few pictures of cats, a couple of badly framed sunsets, and, yes, pictures of socks.

Unusual socks. Pictures of him sitting down or standing,

with his pants riding a little high and colorful socks appearing. Patterns, cartoons, all sorts of things.

I quickly swipe to Google his age. Seventeen, like me. Technically, a month older.

I shake my head, a little horrified at the most unprofessional Instagram account I've ever seen. I go back through his pictures—too many by industry standards, since most publicists will tell you to keep only the most liked pics. A few behind-the-scenes shots on set, a few from actual plays, and no more than four red carpet pics, one of them from the day we met.

William looks different from what I remember, standing tall with his chin up and a charming yet slightly crooked smile. Also slightly crooked? His nose. But he has a birthmark on his right cheek that makes him almost . . . cute. He's wearing a black suit with a white shirt underneath, and there they are: the colorful socks. I zoom in on the image as best as I can, and the big pixels show me it's some sort of cartoon.

I zoom out.

He has a nice smile, I suppose.

I check his tagged pictures.

There are so many pictures with friends that actually seem like friends. Non-famous friends.

I click the face of one of the young girls who's in a lot of his pictures. Her name is Louise Ainsley. She's nine. She's also, apparently, his sister. I don't have any siblings, and all my cousins are about my age or older. After a little cyber-stalking, I find out that William is the second oldest of six children. He has an older sister, who has a son. And apparently they all like each other very, very much, based on how often I see their faces in each other's accounts.

The youngest ones don't have accounts, but everyone else has a public account. Louise is the one with the most posts. She even has a picture of them all on the beach, and a few videos from that day.

I fish the earbuds from the box and put them on as I hold my breath, like I'm a detective doing some very important digging. Then I click on the video.

"UNCLE WILLIAM! Look at the crab!" says a little boy, excitedly pointing at what cannot be a crab and mostly resembles a snail.

William has Louise on his back, so he sits down heavily on the sand and she lands in the water, laughing hysterically. *"It's not a crab, Pete. Mum, Pete doesn't know what a crab is!"* she says.

William laughs and the video cuts out. I let it play again.

I swipe to the next video of the post. It's a continuation. William turns around to see Louise, at this point happily running into the water, and yells, *"It's a different kind of crab, that's all. Pete made a discovery, Lou!"*

The camera shifts to the front, and an older woman with wet hair shakes her head with a loving but knowing expression. The video ends, and then it starts again.

There's something there. The moment he turns around. His bright green eyes laughing into the camera. His back exposed like that. He's skinny, but his shoulders are broader than I expected.

He's not going to be nominated for Hottest Actor of the Year like Trent was four times in a row—he won last year— but he's . . . There's something charming to his lack of build, I suppose. I could see why someone might find him attractive. Not me, but someone out there surely might.

I smile to myself.

What are you doing, Natalia? Stalking a nine-year-old on IG?

I roll my eyes. I want to follow him back, just because. But I also know that there are fan accounts that track everything I do and post screenshots on Twitter. And I don't know if I want them to know that I'm online again.

Now, this is something I should've done already: as-sessed the situation by checking those accounts. I can al-ways count on them to tell me where I've been and what I've done.

I leave Instagram open on Louise Ainsley's account— more specifically, paused on William's back—and go to Twitter. I download it again. As the little image loads, that logo bird stares back at me like it's a challenge. Even with-out eyes, that bird has a powerful stare.

I tell myself I'm not here to check Trent's outings and who he's been talking to or what memes he's been liking.

I'm not here to check William's Twitter profile, either, because that'd be *too* stalkery. (Mostly because I have a tendency of accidentally liking things on Twitter. Its layout is not stalker-friendly.)

I am only here to check my fan accounts and see what they've been up to.

I know the one to go to as soon as the app updates. I ignore the notifications and tap on the search bar. I click @WeStanNat.

The latest tweet reads:

> **BUY NATALIE'S TOGETHER FOREVER ON ITUNES**
>
> **@WeStanNat:**
> OFFICIAL ANNOUNCEMENT: i don't care who you are, if you're using the hashtag #NataFlop to talk trash about our queen, unfollow me right now. let's burn that hashtag!!! who's with me to start #NataQueen?

I stare at that tweet for a second too long. There are two hashtags I could click. I know what will be in the second—pictures of me onstage, GIFs of my music videos and shows. But the first hashtag . . . it's a mystery.

One that I'm dying to uncover. Even if I know it won't be good for me.

I close my eyes and click the hashtag.

I'm prepared for the worst. At least I think I am, anyway.

It turns out I am not.

Someone has made a drawing of me, but they weren't a fan, because I'm crying copiously while Trent smacks a kiss on some hot model—who I assume is meant to be Reese—by his side. The second-most-liked tweet is a GIF of me pointing my finger at his chest and screaming at him. The caption is CRAZY EX-GIRLFRIEND GOT A REMAKE.

Then they get meaner.

I click the first video.

It's me receiving my award, right after Trent dumped me. I'm walking onstage with a forced smile and panda eyes, my makeup all but gone. The presenter awkwardly hands me the small trophy. I raise it and, holding back sobs, say, "I'd like to thank . . . everyone, really! Thank you so much!"

Speech gone. All dignity gone, too, apparently.

When the video ends, a white girl with perfect makeup appears onscreen, laughing hysterically. For thirty seconds straight. Then she stops, shaking her head, saying, "I can't, I can't! *Thank you so much!*" When she mimics my voice, it sounds strangled and whiny.

The eight-year-old in me with fists balled and jaw clenched wants to respond. She really, really wants to respond.

I thought . . . I thought I could handle this. I thought it would go away.

I don't want to cry in Bobbi's office, so I bite the insides of my cheeks as a reminder that I can bite it all back and be who everyone wants me to be. Still be good. Still be graceful. Still be . . . something.

As I glare at my notepad—which is essentially blank—the weight in my chest gets heavier, and my vision blurs.

I force-close Twitter. I force-close Instagram, too.

Linda probably doesn't notice me rubbing my eyes with the backs of my hands, but if she does, she's nice enough to let it slide.

The door opens, and Ashley and Christopher emerge. She gives me a parting smile as they head for the exit.

I fumble to stand up.

Now they're both looking at me.

"I—" I clear my throat, straightening my shoulders. "Ashley, Christopher, I'm sorry, but can you please stay for another half hour? I . . . I changed my mind. I'm in."

Chapter 6

*

Really Sad

"You don't get it," I tell Mom for what feels like the thousandth time.

We've just pulled into the parking lot of my favorite nail salon, but I know we're locked in this car for as long as Mom wishes. She rolls her eyes at me, saying something in Portuguese that I don't quite catch. Tomorrow I'm going back to the office to sign the final papers, and I want to look my best. Then we'll set up the first date, and . . . if I have my nails done, I'll be more confident in *this*. Everything *this* is—my attempt to restore my reputation, my fake boyfriend . . .

"Nati, you can still say no to this."

"To the boyfriend or the outfit?" I ask, gesturing at my cute polka-dot dress. "This is vintage fifties!"

Mom lets out an exasperated laugh. At least I still know how to push her buttons.

"Both." She presses her lips together, then shakes her head. "We're going for mani-pedis! You didn't need to come dressed up like this." I cross my legs, self-conscious. "And the boyfriend? There's definitely still time. You don't need this."

"That's where you're wrong. Double wrong."

As soon as I say it, I watch her face change. It doesn't matter how many albums I've sold, how many awards I have on the living room bookshelf, or how much money I've made. You don't say your Brazilian mother is wrong. You may imply it, but to say it so boldly?

I backtrack.

"It's not that you are wrong, per se," I start. "It's just that maybe you don't have a very broad perspective on this. You still think that I'm beautiful in whatever I wear, and you also think I'll be famous forever no matter what I do. Neither of these things is necessarily true."

Her face softens.

Nailed it.

She runs her hands through her hair, letting out a little breath of frustration.

"Filha, you're unique the way you are. I don't get why you straighten your hair."

I frown. *That?* I've been doing it for forever. I touch my

hair, a dark curtain cascading over my shoulder. I try to mimic her and run my hands through it, but it's already difficult, too many knots. "I—I like it this way."

"Hmm."

We look at each other for a moment.

Then I break into an awkward smile, full-on ignoring what she said before.

"Plus the boyfriend thing, you shouldn't worry. Bobbi assured me that it's legal and that there's no way anyone will find out. She's done this before a thousand times or whatever." I shrug.

She hesitates for a moment. I wonder if she's trying to pick her battles.

"It's not you getting sued that I'm worried about. Do you at least know this boy?"

"God, no." I laugh. "That'd be a nightmare. It's so much better that it's someone I don't know. Less embarrassing that way."

She flashes me a strange look. "You prefer to date a stranger? Trent was your first boyfriend."

She doesn't get it. She just doesn't.

I part my lips to say for the eleventh time that it's not really dating, when she stops me, putting up a hand. "I know what you're going to say. But it's weird that you're going to pretend to date someone you don't know."

"In case *you* don't know, Mom, my reputation isn't at

its best right now. I don't even know anyone famous who'd date me at this point."

She groans. "Fake-date."

I nod. "Fake-date. So they found someone from France, I think? This guy who's super desperate to be famous in the States, so his agent practically begged them for the opportunity or something. Really sad."

I inspect my nails. They've seen better days. I'm wondering how black will look on them. Too goth?

"Really sad," she repeats with a funny tone.

"Really sad," I agree. "That he'd go to these lengths just to get famous, you know."

She snorts. I don't see why.

"One more thing before we go in the salon, baby." She uses her serious tone. The tone for one of two things: business that she'll forbid me to do, or family. I hope it's the first. "Vovó called. She invited us to spend Christmas in São Paulo."

I clear my throat, keep staring at my nails.

"Oh. You don't want to stay in LA, the two of us? It's our tradition."

"Just like you want to spend Christmas with your mother, I want to spend Christmas with mine. Vovó is getting older. And she hasn't seen you outside a television screen in too long." Mom opens the car door, signaling the end of the conversation. "We're going."

I get out of the car, too.

But I'm already thinking of how I can plot my way out of this.

×

The next day, there's a hush when I enter Bobbi's office. Bobbi, Ashley, and Christopher all stop and do a double take, taking in Natalie, the pop star. Not Natalia Rocha, the ruined social outcast whose dignity has gone down the drain. No, I can tell they see the reason why I became so famous. On top of my songwriting, that is.

My smile, my charm, my confident stride, my perfectly manicured nails, my favorite pantsuit by Valentino, all white, but we don't call it *white*. We call it *ice*. The color is *ice*. I love that.

"Good afternoon, friends," I announce, and keep on smiling.

Because it's a good day to be alive. It's a good day to have my reputation restored, too. Ashley clears her throat and looks away, visibly jealous of my spark. She elbows her assistant.

I'm smirking when Bobbi approaches me and whispers, "You have something in your teeth, Natalie."

. . . Oh.

"It's next to your left upper canine. Did you have salad?"

I nod, trying to scrape my embarrassment away with my nail. When I show my teeth to Bobbi, she nods that I'm successful, then kisses my cheek.

"All right," Bobbi announces, then points at the white couch so I can take a seat. I do, still smiling, because nothing will bring me down today. "Rumors have already been planted, all the tabloids are speculating. Ashley has pulled several strings." Bobbi pauses, almost like she's going to raise an imaginary glass to Ashley, but ends up giving her a thumbs-up. "Your boyfriend will arrive here tomorrow. We'll have a car pick him up and you two will meet in a café immediately after that. Ashley has a team who will photograph you and then sell the pictures to the tabloids."

"Oh, okay."

This is fast.

I start asking who it is, but Ashley speaks first.

"The paperwork has been signed on his side, and you'll sign it today, too, so we have the guarantee of privacy, should either of you choose to break the contract," Ashley says. "Although I can't imagine why you would. It's a very lucrative contract for both of your careers. No need to feel nervous about this."

Well, I wasn't feeling nervous *before*.

I clear my throat. "Okay, so . . . who is it? So I can Google him. If he's too tall, maybe I should buy some new heels? Trent was tall, but—maybe you're going full-on basketball player on me, yeah?" I laugh at that. Then I add, "But for a basketball player—no, never mind, he wants Hollywood, so he's an actor. Or is he?" I narrow my eyes. "But is he that tall? I don't think I have shoes for a really tall man."

"Hold your horses, love." Bobbi frowns. "Not a man. A boy. You're seventeen."

"You know what I mean," I say.

Ashley crosses her legs to the opposite side, in the direction of the door. I read in a body language book once about how that means the person really wants to leave. I try to offer her my version of a genuine smile, this time without any lettuce. Ashley smiles back, but it looks more like a grimace.

"We've got the name right here," Ashley says, then eyes her assistant. "Christopher?" He goes through his papers quickly—and my heartbeat speeds up—before announcing:

"Ainsley." And then, dooming it all to hell: "William Ainsley."

"No," I gasp.

Christopher doesn't seem to hear me. "He's been in four movies, all of them small indie productions, but the action movie where he plays the younger brother of the lead, *Becoming the Impossible,* has won quite a few awards. He was nominated for best supporting actor."

He starts talking about net worth, but my throat is dry. I blink a few more times, trying not to sink in my chair.

"That— I'm sorry to interrupt you, but isn't he French?" I turn to Bobbi, indignant.

Bobbi raises an eyebrow. "I never said French. I said European."

My nostrils flare, and I feel a headache coming.

Ashley presses her glasses against the bridge of her nose. "So you know this boy?"

"I—sort of. Not really. Maybe?" I frown. "But he's so . . . scrawny. And pale. And soft." I glare at Bobbi, as if somehow she would understand. "And British. He is British."

"I don't understand. Those are all things that will look good for you right now, Natalie." Ashley glances meaningfully at Christopher, and I can tell this is their signal to wrap things up. He starts organizing his papers. "You don't need another womanizer with a James Dean complex. William Ainsley is the anti-Trent. You need him."

Every word she's said is a nightmare.

As she stands up, I stand up, too.

"I don't need him. He needs me."

Ashley studies me as if I'm a child. "You need him just as badly, Natalie. Don't you want to rise above? We want you to."

Christopher goes over his papers and promptly offers me the contract to be signed. I'd read a copy sent by email, and Bobbi's lawyer has already read it, too, so all I have to do is sign. This time, William Ainsley's name is in the place of "Fake Romantic Partner."

To his benefit, Christopher does shoot me an apologetic look when I take the paper from his hand. I sit on Bobbi's desk, and all eyes are on me.

My hand hovers over the page. Every cell in my body is telling me to flee the scene, and I'm seriously considering asking for a bathroom break. Bobbi clears her throat, glaring at me, and when our eyes meet, it's like she's saying, *What's taking you so long?*

I reply with my eyes: *I really thought he'd be stranger!*

"I guess not." I groan.

The "sign here" written in pencil at the bottom of the page stares at me.

"Sorry?" Ashley asks.

I shake my head. "Oh no, I was talking to myself."

Holding my breath, I sign my name. Then I take a check from my wallet and sign that, too: a check for my pretend-boyfriend, a boost of encouragement for him to act real nice and boyfriend-y while respecting the NDAs. I try to do it as fast as I can, like ripping off a Band-Aid, and when Christopher collects both, he mouths, *Sorry.*

Ashley and Bobbi exchange hopeful looks.

"Yay?" I try to contribute.

I guess I'm dating William Ainsley.

Chapter 7

Don't Look Around

I'm not nervous about having a blind date with a stranger. I *am* nervous about inviting paid photographers to spread a lie—and about being seen with someone I'm not sure my fans would approve of seeing me with. I'm almost positive they'd expect someone . . . bigger. Stronger. Better?

I could barely sleep last night. I was back on William's Instagram, going through all his pictures. And I'm right—he *is* scrawny. All awkward limbs and too pale and so impossibly . . . Well, Ashley was right when she said he's the anti-Trent. Definitely no James Dean complex there.

I'm not sure how that is a good thing. Everyone *loves* James Dean.

Three months. Three months of fake dating, just to distract the tabloids until hopefully I write some new music, and they forget the fiasco. Three months of being photographed beside him and attending at least one or two events with him.

Three months, then, come December, I'm free.

I check my phone, my leg bouncing again under the table outside the cute café. Twitter notifications are off, but I go through some fan accounts anyway. They're talking about the rumors of William and me. There are pictures of each of us side by side with theories about how and when we've met, and whether we're together or not.

We're about to prove to everyone that we are (in fact, liars).

I start reading an interesting account of my possible romance with William. It says there were eyewitnesses of our first meeting in Moscow, me running in the rain to get to the hotel, and him finding me and letting me use his jacket as an umbrella. We laughed together as we made our way to the hotel. Me, stopping hesitantly in the lobby. Eventually taking a pen from the reception desk and running back to him shyly, writing my number on his arm, then running up to the elevator with a wink.

There is a number of inconsistencies with this story, mainly that I have never been to Russia, and how incredibly out of character it would have been for me to do the whole shy thing. But it's a meet-cute, and it's probably good that so many people are retweeting it. A good meet-cute could make or break a ship. I wonder if Ashley had any hand in planting this story.

I lock my phone and let out a sigh.

And then hands cover my eyes.

I jump, yelling and slapping the hands away.

William Ainsley laughs, stepping out from behind me, and says, "Okay, then."

I scan the crowd. Ashley's people are definitely here; I can see someone behind the bushes across the street.

"You scared me." I force a smile between gritted teeth.

"Sorry," William says, not looking sorry.

He's obviously come straight from the airport, and judging by the dark circles around his eyes, he hasn't slept much more than I have. Yet, unlike me, he probably hasn't dedicated a good portion of an hour to makeup and concealer. On top of stylist-approved makeup, I'm also wearing a black crop top with a high-waisted denim skirt with a black belt. Casually cute. Besides the ring I always wear with my initial, I chose a delicate necklace with a small teardrop sapphire. And boots. Wonderfully comfortable boots, for once.

He's fresh-faced, not a hint of stubble on that chin. But he isn't *too bad*. In black skinny jeans and an Arctic Monkeys T-shirt, I'd maybe place him as a rocker wannabe if I saw him at a festival or something. Definitely not an actor. That part still doesn't make sense to me.

William pauses, shifting his weight from one foot to the other.

"Your agent told me to kiss your cheek or something. Because. Pictures."

I stare up at him.

He seems so absolutely out of place, hands tucked into the pockets of his jeans, that I start doubting Ashley's effectiveness at having found someone fitting for a fake-dating business.

"I'll do it," I say.

I want the best shot possible for those photographers in the bushes—why the hell are they even in the bushes when we asked them to be there?—so I get up and touch his shoulders. He turns to me. His green eyes widen, and I press a kiss on his lips.

I pause, so it can be caught on camera.

He smells good. And he moves his soft lips just a little bit against mine.

My firm grip on his shoulders softens, and I'm about to let my hands slide down to his biceps when I remember what's happening and pull away. Opening my eyes, I clear my throat and sit down again.

"There. You wouldn't be kissing my cheek if we were really dating."

William's lips quirk, and he murmurs, "Well, *I* didn't want to be the person to rush into this with a kiss, out of nowhere. But I guess you do things differently here in the States?"

Is that supposed to be a joke? Is he trying to be cute?

Three months of this. Oh, Lord, give me strength.

Self-consciously, I try to make my hair look straighter by combing through it with my fingers. He raises his hand to the waiter and asks for a lemonade. I already have a smoothie in front of me.

William frowns, staring at the glass table between us. "So. Do you want to talk about this?"

I give him an equally self-conscious smile. "Smile. You're having a great time with your beloved girlfriend." The words feel strangled, and I almost want to laugh at this absurd situation. "And for the love of God, only whisper when you talk about it. We don't want anyone eavesdropping."

William looks around.

"Don't look around!" I whisper-yell.

He widens his eyes again, staring at me. "Okay, I'm not looking around, fine." He shows his teeth. "Smiling. Having a good time." He lowers his voice an octave, "With my surprise girlfriend."

I breathe out slowly. "I don't think you should've accepted this deal. I know it's good for you, but, honestly? It's weird because we have sort of already met."

"As opposed to how normal it would feel otherwise?" he

teases as his lemonade arrives. "It's all right, I'm not entirely comfortable with this, either. But Cedrick—my agent—is sure that it's going to be mutually beneficial, so." He lifts his shoulders. "I have to say that . . . I'm sorry, by the way. I'm really sorry about what happened. Nobody deserves that kind of treatment."

I scan him for lies, but so far, the only thing that's fake here is our relationship. I nod, not really wanting to get into it, but he presses on.

"Your boyfriend really is an arse. He shouldn't have done that to you." He shakes his head, then takes a sip of his lemonade. I cock an eyebrow, forgetting to smile. He corrects himself, "I'm sorry. Ex-boyfriend, of course."

I want to say I don't need his kindness, but instead I say, "Clearly you're *superior* to my ex."

Ignoring my sarcasm, he makes a face. "I mean, I'd seen some of his movies. He *always* struck me as an arse, and I am a good judge of character, I guess," he says. I have the impression he's only half joking. "Also, I'm no expert or anything, but shouldn't you have deleted your ex's pictures from Insta already? I deleted mine. Cedrick told me to."

Which means he recently got out of a relationship as well. I wonder what she's like. Is she also a Londoner like him? Someone hyper family-oriented and quirky, who likes socks or . . . I don't know, *beanies*?

Then, after a beat: "I mean, I'm not trying to tell you what to do. Obviously. It's just that I've already deleted my photos, so I thought it'd be weird if you still had yours. But, again, up to you."

Then, his phone rings. I want to call him out on how unprofessional it is that his phone isn't on silent mode during a business meeting—because kiss or not, that is what this is: a business meeting. But then he takes out his phone, and I can read the screen: BIG SIS. His brow furrows, and he clears his throat, standing up. "Sorry, I have to take this. I'll be back in a second."

I watch him leave without saying a word.

So much for keeping this professional.

I take out my phone as well and go on Instagram to give myself something to do while I wait. Because he's right; I should delete my pictures with Trent. But I hate every single moment of it. I hate it because deleting pictures with thousands of likes feels like a setback. I hate it because deleting pictures with Trent feels a lot like deleting what I've accomplished, too.

I put my phone on the table like the opposite of a call for truce and wait for him to come back. He does, distressed and disheveled, hair messed like he's run his hand over his head a gazillion times.

Then I remember, *again*. The first time we met, the things he said . . . But here he is, cashing in on a celebrity and fake-dating her, too. Chin tilted up, I say matter-of-factly, "Turns out you don't think *all* of the industry is stupid."

William's brows come together for a second, then he grins. "I'm detecting some anger. What could I possibly have done to warrant this level of annoyance?"

Nostrils flared, I tell him, "I just think you're pretentious. With your"—I gesture at him—"attitude or something. Your pretentious indie-movie-star attitude and being oh-so-sorry about what happened with Trent."

"I see." He nods. "You'd rather I was glad about what happened that day? Should I be wearing a leather jacket and boots, perhaps? Next time, tell me what you want, and I'll be that. We're chameleons, we pretentious indie-movie stars." He raises his glass.

I breathe out as slowly as I can. "You don't take me seriously."

"I take you for a self-obsessed diva who's not ready to ask for help even when she needs it," he deadpans. I scoff, but he's doing that thing where he sort of grins. "I'm not saying I don't need help, too. I do. I signed this contract, Natalia, and I want this to work out. I need this to work out."

Wait.

"What did you just call me?"

The attitude drops. He blinks, confused, and shifts uncomfortably in his seat. "I . . . your name? It said 'Natalia' in the contract."

I bite the insides of my cheeks and try to sound calm when I speak.

"It's *Natalie*," I say, forcing the American accent. "That's my name."

He studies me for a second. Those dark green eyes take me apart and put me back together again. Finally, he nods, and he's back to focusing all his attention on the lemonade.

I feel something tug at my insides.

Why did I agree to this?

I start playing with my phone, my black nails digging at the protective case.

William reaches across the table and covers my hand with his. "Are you okay?"

His thumb caresses the back of my hand with the lightest of touches.

I can't seem to tear my eyes away from our hands.

I have a question about to roll off my tongue, something along the lines of *why do you care?* And a not-small part of me wants to open up and tell him everything I'm feeling right now. Then I catch movement in the corner of my eye, and I hear the click of the camera.

I taste something bitter in my mouth.

Smart boy. He's learning fast, giving the cameras a good show.

I pull my hand back as smoothly as I can, and give him a bright smile as I answer, "Never better."

Chapter 8

Unless Asked Nicely, Of Course

The one time I need Mom not to be home, she is.

I'm standing in front of the red door of our apartment like a stalker. I can just barely hear her sing as she cooks something. I groan, pressing my forehead to the door. Instead of taking out my keys, I take out my phone, wanting to stall this moment. She's going to ask me about the *date*, and I . . . don't want to have this conversation right now.

I have lots of notifications. Artists are following me on Instagram again. I roll my eyes at that and delete the notifications with a swipe. I go to my text messages. There are unread messages from Bobbi, Brenda, and an unknown number.

I open the unknown number first.

> **UNKNOWN NUMBER:**
>
> Hi! This is your pretentious indie-movie-star pretend-boyfriend.
>
> Thought you should have my American number.
>
> Apparently I'll be around for a bit.

The message doesn't change the longer I stare at my screen. I press my lips together, trying to think of a way to reply, a way that isn't as stiff as I probably was today, but one that isn't too *something else*, either.

I don't know what I'm thinking.

God.

I close my eyes and say the only swear word I know in Portuguese. "Merda."

I decide to reply to William later. My mind's already enough of a mess after our fake-date today. Or, well, our date with fake intentions. Whatever. I open up the next text.

> **BOBBI:**
>
> Super sorry Ashley's photographers were too late to get you guys on camera
>
> Hope it was a fun date anyway?

I frown. I take a step back from the door, staring at the message for a long minute.

Someone was taking pictures. And if it wasn't Ashley's photographers . . .

I select Brenda's text.

A picture with a link, followed by "WTF."

The picture is of me, sitting outside a flowery coffee shop, with an honest-to-God enraged expression on my face, slapping William's hands away as he stands behind me, shocked and afraid.

I click the link to a tabloid website.

It reads: TROUBLE IN PARADISE ALREADY?

Already.

"No, no, no, no, no."

I save William's number quickly so I can forward the picture to him. I follow it with a string of worried and unhappy emojis.

I click on the link again. Zoom in on his terrified face. My scowl. Then, inexplicably, my fingers zoom in on his feet. I hadn't realized it when we were together, but he was wearing bright blue socks with black polka dots.

The screen goes dark for a moment, and I nearly throw my phone against the wall when it starts vibrating in my hand.

BRITISH BOYFRIEND, the screen says. Calling me.

What kind of person actually *calls* people?

The phone won't stop vibrating, and his name won't go away, so I let out a deep sigh and take the call.

Resting my back against the front door, I say, "Hello?"

"Hi, um, Natalie," he begins, as eloquently as ever. "So I saw what you sent me."

"Good. I sent it to you so you'd see it."

He's quiet on the other end of the call. This is why texting is a thousand times better.

I clear my throat. "Turns out it wasn't Ashley's photographers. It was real paparazzi, and they took some unflattering pictures of us."

William groans on the other end, then groans some more. There's a rustle as if he's moving. I'm struck with the image of him rolling out of bed, then shake my head.

"Yeah. I did seem terrified." He laughs.

He has a nice laugh. Low, throaty.

"I hate to state the obvious, but you're not supposed to be scared of me. You're supposed to be *in love* with me."

"I could be both," he teases. "All we have to do is make up for it. Show that we're fine, and you don't usually slap me too much."

I open and close my mouth.

"Unless I ask nicely, of course," he adds.

I feel my cheeks burning hot. "Ugh, don't."

William laughs again on the other end of the call, and I can't help but smile. Something about his laugh releases the pressure a tiny bit. "Don't worry, okay? This is nothing. You've been in the public eye for longer: What would you do to fix this situation if it weren't *your* situation?"

My immediate reaction is to tell him that I'd call Bobbi.

But that isn't true. If it wasn't mine, if I didn't have the obligation to fix it . . .

"Mmmm." I suck in my bottom lip, looking up at the high ceiling of the foyer. "Pretend like it didn't happen. Wait a few days and post a cute picture on Instagram. Maybe do a story of a date?"

He's silent for a second. Then, "Are you asking me on a date?"

"I— What? No, I wasn't—" I sputter.

William cuts me off, chuckling. "Then I am asking you. Let's go on a date and make sure people are jealous of how happy we are, and how not at all scared I am."

My lips quirk, and my hand goes to the pendant around my neck, absentmindedly turning it in my fingers.

"Under one condition, of course," William says, his voice a little lower. "No more slapping?"

I'm so unprepared for that, it actually makes me snort with laughter.

"See? You already knew what to do."

I lean against the door, wondering if William's smiling on the other end.

Suddenly, I'm falling.

The door opens inward, and my arms pinwheel as I land flat on my back with a yelp.

My phone jumps out of my hand and clatters across the floor. I can hear William's voice, yelling, "Natalie? What happened? Natalie?!"

Mom gives me a strange look, still holding the door open.

I scramble to grab my phone and bring it to my ear again. "Everything's fine. I have to hang up now. Goodbye." Before he can say anything, I end the call. "Mother." I give her a nod.

Mom's frown grows deeper. "Why were you outside? Why didn't you come in? Did you forget your keys? Why didn't you knock?"

I blink at her. "Gosh, so many questions. I—I was about to come in."

"Was that Bobbi? Because she called me and said she was trying to get in touch with you. Something about the tabloids or—" She stops there, shrugging.

Mom's view of my image is that I don't have one outside of who I am as an artist. Which is why she's been dropping hints here and there about me going back to the studio.

"No, I—I'll call her back. I know what she wants. And it'll be an amazingly short call, because that's what people do. They say what they need to and hang up." I put my phone in the pocket of my skirt and start toward my bedroom. "It's how society works."

Mom hums. "How was the date?"

"Not a date!" I yell from the stairs. "Not a date," I say again, this time to myself. "None of this is real."

The second I'm safely inside my room, my phone beeps again. It's William. My eyes widen, and I clutch the phone to my chest for a second before sliding my thumb over the screen.

> **BRITISH BOYFRIEND:**
> Please send proof of life.

I snort, open the front camera, and start toward the bed. As I flop onto it, I receive another message:

> **BRITISH BOYFRIEND:**
> Just because, you know. It sounded like
> something happened.
> Something deadly.

I slide up the notification so I'm staring at myself in the front selfie camera. My hair is all around my head like a dark halo, and I tilt my head to the side in a way that I know makes my neck look longer as I snap a photo.

Clicking the gallery, I inspect the picture.

It's so staged.

But I still like it.

I hit *send*, drop the phone to my chest, and close my eyes. Almost immediately, it beeps, and I pick it up again.

> **BRITISH BOYFRIEND:**
> Good.

> Because I think I've got our next date
> planned out.

I roll over onto my elbows on the bed, and reread his message again. And again. I send a winky emoji back.

Trent wasn't big on dates, at least not ones he planned. His agent, Carrie, was good at that sometimes. She even sent me roses on my birthday. But the dates were always at very public places, so we could be seen together. It wasn't that Trent didn't like hanging out with me, but if he could do it *and* boost our social media presence? Two birds with one stone.

Not that William isn't doing it to boost our social media presence, too.

I sit up, my brow furrowed at the screen. He's just being strategic. He probably called his agent or publicist for help, too. Business transaction and all.

As soon as I kick off my boots, I lie back on the bed again, phone in my hands. I open the group chat with the girls.

> **NATALIE:**
> so the situation with the pic will be fixed

> **PADMA:**
> what situation?

BRENDA:
thank god
i'll fill you in later bb

PADMA:
okay? lol

BRENDA:
SO HOW IS HE???? SPILL THE TEA!!!!!

NATALIE:
hold on, i'll send a pic
<williamainsley5720S7D.jpg is sent>

BRENDA:
did u just have that saved
that was a very quick send

PADMA:
awww he's cute! in a boyish kind of way
so obviously i'm not attracted

BRENDA:
let the bi speak!!!!!
HE'S CUTE

PADMA:

just bc i'm a lesbian i can't have a sense of
aesthetics?

pls

NATALIE:

ANYWAY . . . cute isn't what i wanted tho

i wanted HOT

DELICIOUS

FIERCE

i wanted . . . someone even better than
trent

better-looking, at least

generally better wouldn't be very hard

BRENDA:

u don't know him that well yet

maybe he'll surprise you ;)

PADMA:

ew

NATALIE:

gross

BRENDA:

u guys suck

PADMA:

is your fake boyfriend nice though? can
you at least be friends?

NATALIE:

what do you mean >at least<?
that was the plan from day 1

BRENDA:

today is day 1

PADMA:

don't overcomplicate things, stop being
you!!!!
i'm just asking if he's nice

NATALIE:

he's full of himself honestly
he thinks he's better than me

PADMA:

why do you say that?

NATALIE:

he called me a diva

PADMA:

oh

BRENDA:

i already love him

NATALIE:

not funny

he said i was self-obsessed

and didn't know how to ask for help??

or something like that idk

BRENDA:

i would die for this beautiful british fool

PADMA:

are you upset that he has onions

sorry autocorrect, opinions**

NATALIE:

he can have all the stinky onions he wants

idc

i'm upset that you two are terrible friends

who won't side with me

but i'll let it slide

anyway how was your day??

PADMA:

spent at the studio. recorded a new single

i guess

we'll see how my producer feels about it

ricky hasn't been giving me much love

lately

BRENDA:

i'm still pretending i don't have to apply to

any colleges

so that's been fun

NATALIE:

you're both brilliant

ricky is going to love the single

& the college thing is all right, you have time

PADMA:

fhdiosgs hopefully

BRENDA:

and you?

NATALIE:

what do you mean?

BRENDA:

what's on /your/ mind?

NATALIE:

that maybe i should go to college

and maybe never sing again

or should i go to the studio

and make some actual music

maybe college

yeah i'm feeling good about going to

college and dropping my musical career so

i don't have to write anything new

I stare at our chat for a moment. Then, without giving it much thought, I force-close the app and open the Notes app. I start a new file and tell myself out loud, "This doesn't have to be a song. You're writing down your thoughts about . . . this weird limbo feeling. No pressure."

As I draft no-pressure-these-don't-have-to-be-lyrics, it's William's face that's on my mind.

Chapter 9

Say Cheese

Ashley has a car sent to pick me up, and the drive takes so long I run out of things to look at on Pinterest. I've been trying to stay on there, looking at pretty motivational phrases and cat pictures, instead of hopping over to Twitter or Instagram. It helps with the FOMO.

The driver introduces himself as Sean, then doesn't say another word for an hour. We arrive in a rural area, and I ask Sean if this is really the place. But he only gives me a side-eye glance through the rearview mirror. I guess I wouldn't have liked anyone to ask me mid-performance if I know how to do my job, either.

"I hope you dressed for a picnic," Sean says.

I am most definitely *not* dressed for a picnic.

I'm wearing a solid yellow crop top and a black-and-brown-plaid skirt that's going to be riding a bit too high if we have to sit down. William did mention we'd be going out of town, but I didn't expect *this*.

"Great," I murmur.

Finally, he stops the car. "I can't go any farther. The road ends here." He turns back to face me. "You go up that hill, you see? With the big tree?" He points. I do see. And it's very far.

"Beyond that tree there's a valley on the other side of the hill, so anyone standing at the top has a clear view and can take good pictures. I think the photographers will arrive soon."

"Do I have to walk? All the way up there *and then down?*"

He raises an eyebrow. I just know in my heart that he's holding back from saying something like *you can try flying* but is trying to be professional. I put him out of his misery by nodding and getting out of the car.

Before I leave, he says, "I'll be waiting right here when you're ready."

"Thanks," I say, before slamming the door of the car by accident. "Sorry!" I call out, but if he hears me, he makes no motion to acknowledge my apology.

Nervous, slippery hands.

I sigh and stare up at the hill, the heat of the sun scorching my face. Should've put my hair up in a ponytail or something. If I sweat, my hair will start curling desperately. Damn, I hope William's already waiting for me.

By the time I've reached the tree, I'm sweating and gross and want to sit down.

"Natalie?" William jogs up to meet me.

He's grinning from ear to ear. Like this is fun. Or funny. I don't even know. "To be honest, I thought for a moment that you were standing me up. That I might be deserted out here. I maaaaay have eaten most of the apple pie. Desperate times, you know?"

I shake my head but can't help the smile tugging at my lips.

Mentally preparing for the upcoming kiss we will invariably have, I rest against the tree and try to cool off. William offers me his hand for support. I take it, cursing my choice to wear ankle boots. The thick heels seem to be swallowed by the grass with every step. But no kiss.

He chuckles, giving me a once-over. "Don't you have a stamina trainer or something for your dance routines?"

"I have a personal trainer who's focused on stamina, yes, but it's for my breath." My voice does sound steady even though I might as well be dying. "I'm not a dancer."

I don't know how I feel about the fact that he's probably never watched one of my performances. Disappointed, maybe? I've barely gotten over that he didn't know who I was when I was nominated—and won!—Female Artist of the Year, but now I'm his fake girlfriend and the fact that he still hasn't seen me perform is off-putting.

I don't look back at him until we reach the blanket and picnic basket waiting for us spread under another tree, maybe twelve feet high. This tree is full of white blossoms, as is much of the park, but this one feels special. It feels like . . . our tree? No, that's silly. This is a fake date, after all.

But it's beautiful here. So much green, so much nature. It feels like we're transported to another world for a few hours.

"So you're not very athletic," he deadpans.

Turning to him with a semi-offended expression, I finally take in what he's wearing. A soft white T-shirt under a light-blue plaid shirt with ripped jeans that are ripped just enough that I can see his thighs.

They're . . . nice. He looks really cool. I especially like the plaid.

He's kicked off his sneakers and is wearing socks with clovers on them. Interesting and a fitting choice for this setting.

William seems like he's waiting for an answer.

"I'm athletic *enough*."

He breaks into a smile and sits on the crimson blanket. He looks like part of the decoration. "I'm a brilliant dancer. I can give you lessons one day if you want."

I narrow my eyes at him.

"I mean it!" he insists.

Choosing to ignore that—because I am *not* going to dance in front of anyone, ever, much less him—I sit down on the blanket as well. The apple pie on top of the closed basket is almost entirely gone.

"This heat is killing me," I murmur, trying to adjust my skirt so it doesn't ride up.

"All smiles, we're on a romantic picnic!" He grins, but even he seems to be finding this ridiculous. He lies down properly, taking the last slice of the apple pie. "Why don't you put your hair up in a bun or something? My sisters do it all the time."

I try to sit with my knees bent and legs angled to the side, but it feels like the fabric of the skirt wasn't made for this. At least I'm in the shade.

"That's horrifying. It can't be good for straightened hair."

William turns to me with both eyebrows raised and pie crumbs around his mouth. "That's not what your hair naturally looks like?"

I shake my head.

"Huh." He frowns, sits up, and starts taking off his plaid shirt. I'm about to ask what the hell he's doing, but I don't have time to make an uncomfortable joke about his striptease before he hands me the shirt, and says, "Here. You can wrap this around your waist. So you can sit however you want. It's not the best, but it'd help, wouldn't it?"

"I—yes. Yes, it will." And a little late, because I'm still not sure what this is, I add, "Thank you."

I know that it won't be super fashionable for the pictures. But at least I can sit. Right now, I'm caring more about the latter.

"Okay." I pull my hair to the side so it doesn't bother me as much. "Our order of the day is taking at least one very good selfie so we can post it to our Instagram accounts, and possibly making some Instagram stories, too, so people can see how spontaneous we are." I waggle my eyebrows at "spontaneous."

William nods. "That. Or we could just eat and talk for a bit, let those people do their jobs and take their pictures, and *then* we can take a few selfies, when it's not too awkward."

"This is not awkward. I'm not feeling awkward."

He smirks. I don't like that smirk.

"I'm not," I insist.

"You're not, I get it. You're perfectly comfortable. Your choice of clothes reflects that rather well." He winks at me. Who even *winks*? He must think he's the lead of a nineties rom-com or something.

He pulls the basket closer and starts going over the contents, putting them on the blanket between us. "I did eat the apple pie, but we also have some strawberries, which I guess is supposed to be sexy?" He makes a funny face. "We also have some nuts, which are definitely not sexy." He places the little plastic container next to the one with strawberries. "A few sandwiches, too. I assume Ashley prepared these herself, with *all* her love," he says, with a hint of sarcasm.

I reach for the container with the sandwiches, and grab

one. The label reads TURKEY SANDWICH BY EDDY'S. I flash him the label, and smile. "No doubt. Ashley definitely handpicks all the food and prepares it herself."

"For all the fake dates," he agrees. "Can I ask you a question?"

Universally speaking, that phrase never precedes anything good. I clutch his shirt a little closer to my waistline and nod, forgetting that I probably shouldn't look this tense for the pictures. But if he notices, he doesn't mention it.

"First time we saw each other, at the awards, before . . . Your handbag fell. And an inhaler fell out of it. I don't want to make any assumptions, but you seemed freaked out."

Oh. Yeah.

That.

I take a deep breath. William's staring at the picnic basket. I look past him at the trees standing tall around us and the grass so freshly cut that everything smells like it.

Tucking some of my hair behind my ears, I say, "I don't really have asthma. But whenever I go to big events, I take an inhaler with me. My first time on *The Late Show*, I couldn't breathe. I was waiting in the greenroom, and I just couldn't for the life of me find my breath. It wasn't asthma. I was nervous. But I remember wishing it was something like asthma, because then it wouldn't be my fault. Just something that couldn't be helped. The inhaler is like a security blanket. It's weird, but I calm down faster when I hold it." I shrug, my eyes still focused on the grass.

But I catch his reaction, the consideration in his eyes and the way he seems uncomfortable. It's like he's fighting a small war with himself on what to say next.

"I'm so sorry—"

I cut him off. "It's okay. It's not like my nerves are your fault." I shrug, hoping my expression makes it come across as no biggie. I add, "The doctor did think I had asthma at first. That's why I have the inhaler. But my voice coach had us follow up with a specialist, and it turns out I didn't."

"Yeah. Was it like an anxiety attack?" he presses.

Was it? I don't know. I never put a name to it.

"Probably, but it doesn't matter, because I hardly need it anymore." Not often. The last time I felt close to losing my breath like that was at the People's Choice Awards.

William studies me in that way of his, like he's taking in every inch of me. Finally he asks, "Did you bring it today?"

"I . . . didn't." I feel like I should probably explain that I only get that nervous at events or big performances or . . . well. I don't know how to explain why I don't have it now. "I don't want anyone to find out about this." *Nobody knows.* Not Bobbi, not Ashley, not Brenda or Padma. Definitely not Trent. Only Mom. And now William, I guess.

He gives me a nod, and then there's that silence between us again, but it isn't like before. It's understanding.

He's quiet and keeps flipping the handle of the basket, unconsciously trying to break it.

"Acting is a big deal for you, isn't it?" I ask.

He looks up at me, and his whole face lights up. "I love it. Yeah. I do take it seriously."

"How did you get involved in that?" I grab another sandwich.

"Oh." William hums. "I was in plenty of school plays. Then one day this old man approached me after a play and I tried to run away because, as you know, children are not supposed to talk to strangers. Turns out he was a scout."

I almost spit out my food. "No way!"

"Yes way," he replies, laughing. "I was maybe nine? What even was in Cedrick's head, to approach a child like that without any parent around? That was bananas."

I think the fact that he says "bananas" is bananas, but I don't say that.

Instead I nod along. "Yeah, I was also scouted. From a talent show. But Bobbi was definitely more professional about it and gave her card to Mom before she even looked my way twice." Realizing I may sound arrogant, I add, "But I'm sure Cedrick is an excellent guy and hasn't crept on pre-adolescent boys since."

"Oh no, not that I know of. Now he's solidly creeping on dogs."

"What!"

"He actually has a new client who's a dog. Apparently, it will be in a big movie next year and all. I can imagine how easy it is to get auditions when everybody wants to pet you." Remorsefully, he adds, "Nobody wants to pet me, Natalie."

For a moment I actually consider petting him. Not because I'd like to feel his dark curls under my hand, I tell myself, but because it'd be good for the pictures.

"So how's fame been for you?" he asks, and then stuffs his mouth with two strawberries at once. Definitely not sexy.

I open and close my mouth, searching for the words.

Empowering. Draining. Incredible. Terrible.

"Fame is complicated. But music . . . music is simple." I shrug. He smiles. A tilted corner-of-mouth type of smile. His big green eyes are encouraging, and before I know it, I'm talking again. "I feel like music is as important to me as *air*. I don't think I can live without it. Wait, is that a total cliché?"

He laughs. "A little cliché. But I get it."

I nod. "Right. There's something magical about having a full arena of fans singing your words. I've written all my songs, and the moment I offer one to the crowd, it feels like we're sharing that epiphany."

William's still sitting with his back a little hunched and the basket between his legs, but I swear it's like the gravity around us changes, pulling us closer together. He doesn't look away and I don't, either.

He slowly nods. "That's special."

I realize something and groan. "So you're probably

wondering about 'Together Forever,' and how stupid I was to write that about Trent and me."

That steals a laugh from him. "I wasn't thinking that at all! But do tell if you want to."

I shrug. "I wrote that song when we first met. He was my first boyfriend. I think I'm entitled to think it was going to be forever, right?" I glance at his shirt over my legs, my hands fidgeting around the edges so I have something to do with myself. "Everyone must be mocking me for that song. Maybe not as much now, since I have a *new boyfriend*." I pause, rolling my eyes. He doesn't laugh this time. "But I did think it'd be forever."

William sighs. "My therapist says that every step on the way forces us to go forward. I get that it can't be fun to have all those people prying into your personal life. But I do believe it's pushing you forward."

I raise my eyebrows. "You have a therapist?"

He frowns. "You haven't got one?"

I'm sure I look like a fish, opening and closing my mouth. Great move, Natalie.

"I—no, I don't. I thought you had to be depressed or something to be in therapy."

William laughs, so fondly that he actually claps, as if that's rich. He puts the basket away, and scoots closer until he's next to me, and looks down at his hands as if guiding my eyes.

"Okay, no, it's like this." He points his index fingers

forward, and moves them in parallel, without them getting close. "It's sort of, this is your mental health, right? And then for a number of reasons—maybe childhood trauma or chemical imbalances or current stress or whatever, doesn't need to be something recent—this happens." He keeps moving one finger at the same pace in a straight line as before, and the other goes a little off, moving in bizarre shapes. I glance away from his fingers and up to his face with an honest-to-God confused expression. This whole finger thing makes no sense. But he's still dedicated to his explanation. "So for you to learn how to deal with those moments better, and keep the pace—" He makes both hands move in a straight line again. "Therapy. Everyone on the planet can benefit from it."

He grins.

"Right," I say. "Um, okay, I admit that maybe if I'd been in therapy when the whole thing blew up, it wouldn't have been as hard. Or so I hope."

He shrugs. "You don't need to wait for the next crisis to go to therapy. I didn't."

I suck my bottom lip in, watching him. He's so close.

I wonder about the traumas he's suffered, and what crises he's averted and which ones he didn't. But I know I'd be intruding if I asked.

Perhaps in an attempt to win his trust somehow, I blurt out, "I don't know my dad."

William raises his eyebrows, but not in a way that's full

of pity. It's like he wasn't expecting it, but he doesn't want to shut me out, either. He gives me a small nod to go on if I want to, and though I don't usually talk about this, I find myself wanting to dive in.

"He left when my mom was pregnant. She was really young, so that wasn't great . . . I mean, I guess. It's not like I was there to see it unfold." I shrug, but the way he looks at me, earnest, tells me that he knows my attempt at humor has more to do with my nervous hands than really wanting to be funny. "Mom raised me. Even when she's busy, it's . . . us. A team."

I can see every shift in his expression.

So much understanding. It makes me feel suspended in time.

William's eyebrow twitches, and he says, "I can't pretend I know what that feels like, but . . . Dad died last year. We were not that close. I was always closer to Mum and my siblings. He was gone a lot, working his office job. But I still miss him."

I want to reach out and squeeze his hand so bad.

It makes me self-conscious of where my hands lie on my thighs.

"I am so sorry—"

He stops me. "It's okay. He was already a bit sick. The part that sucks even more is that it left us in a bunch of debt, between the funeral and the loss of income." He shrugs. "But he was sick, yeah. It gets to a point where you know it's best to say goodbye, that they're just . . . suffering."

I've never had anyone in my family be seriously sick; my grandpa died before I could form any memories of him. Still, I want to show William that I relate, that I understand. How do you show support without knowing how deeply it has affected someone?

Suddenly, his eyes land on me with surprise. "Oh, I'm sorry, you were talking about what happened to you, and I went full blues on you."

The way he says that makes me laugh, and my face warms up. "No, that's okay. Thanks for sharing. I wouldn't have known what to add about my dad leaving, to be honest. It's just something that happened."

"Part of your history, huh?" he asks.

"I'd never thought about it that way, but I guess so, yeah."

We stare at each other for another second.

His eyes search my face for something. I don't know if he finds it, but suddenly his nostrils flare and he clears his throat. "Should we, um, take some selfies?"

I take my phone out. "Say cheese."

Chapter 10

That's What Buddies Do

om doesn't want to watch novelas—too preoccupied with work stuff that she says I can't
help her with—so I'm confined to my bedroom, searching
Netflix for something to watch that won't demand deep
emotional investment.

There's some guilt involved, too. I know I'm supposed
to be writing. I even vaguely know the concepts I want to
explore in my next songs, but as I stare at my guitar sitting
pretty on the other side of the bedroom, I can only groan
and turn back to the Netflix home screen.

I'm on the first five minutes of a gardening reality show
when my phone beeps.

It's Brenda. She sends me a picture with a heart-eyes
emoji.

It's one of the pictures that were "leaked" from the picnic yesterday. William and me sticking our tongues out to take a selfie on my phone, his head resting on my shoulder, my other hand high to angle the picture.

It'd been a little awkward, as we pretended we'd done this a thousand times, but seeing the picture, we look perfectly comfortable and happy.

I close the Messages app and go to my Instagram page to see the pictures we posted. He posted the silly one; I posted one of us smiling at the camera. Super ridiculously staged, but we're so cute. My hair isn't as sweaty, and my makeup is impeccable, subtle enough that it could maybe seem like I'm not wearing any.

A lot of effort goes into looking effortless.

And William . . . he looks good, too. Fluffy, curly hair combed back, as he smiles his slightly crooked smile at the camera. His green eyes are killer.

They get brighter when he's happy.

I go to his page next. The picture of us both sticking our tongues out is his latest post. The caption is a little red heart.

He looks so silly. We both look so silly.

I fall back in bed, holding the phone above me, and go back to some of his other pictures. His stupid socks. His hair that could use a haircut. His love for his family.

I turn around, touching his profile picture for the Instagram story.

On the screen, I see myself rolling my eyes with a smile. He says, "Do it! Please!" and I laugh—not a forced laugh, but a real laugh—before singing the chorus to "God Save the Queen" by the Sex Pistols, shaking my head so my hair goes everywhere.

He cheers. End of video.

"Silly, silly, silly," I repeat out loud, as if for good measure.

I suck on my bottom lip as I go through the numbers. His followers have doubled already. I read the comments, and a quick overview tells me that people are enjoying us together.

A match made in PR agency heaven.

But I refuse to feel weird about this.

This was an important business decision. Bobbi texted me that we're back on top, ironically, with "Together Forever." I need to write new songs. And I also need to stop thinking about all the things I need to do.

I groan and pull the laptop back on my lap. I try watching three more minutes of the reality show, before I put it on pause and open another tab and search "*William Ainsley.*"

The whole first page of results is about us together. One of the headlines is *Everything You Need to Know About Natalie's New Boo.* I click. It mostly talks about him being a British actor of indie movies, that he's won awards, that he's done a lot of volunteer work with children.

I go back to the search page and click through until it's news only about him.

Finally, I find something that makes me pause. It's a link to his *Romeo and Juliet* remake on Amazon Prime.

Mmmm.

Nobody will judge me if nobody knows.

I hit play.

"Morning, sunshine."

For a split second, I think William is waking me up.

Mom doesn't seem to have noticed. She's too busy pulling open all my curtains so forcefully she might rip them. "Morning?" I say, squinting against the sun, trying to regain some of my dignity.

When she's done with the curtains, she comes and sits on the end of my bed. She has that look on her face, like I should guess what she's about to say, but if I try, I'll get it wrong.

"Vovó's birthday is today."

I raise both eyebrows, and my stomach does a little flip thing that isn't cute.

"Oh. That's . . . that's great."

Mom sighs, her shoulders falling. "Why is it so hard for you to call and say feliz aniversário? You don't need to have a fifty-minute conversation. Though she would appreciate that."

I press my lips together.

"It's not that I don't like talking to Vovó. I do. I love her. She's really sweet."

Mom touches my foot over the sheets. "Then what is it? Help me understand why everything about my family is so painful to you."

"No, Mamis, no," I say, crawling to her. I put my hands in hers. "It's not that it's *your family*. I just—and it isn't painful, either—I just know that . . . that I don't fit in. I know what they think of me."

She snorts. "What do they think of you, Natalia?"

My stomach turns. "That I'm a sell-out. That I've given up on being Brazilian to be American. They don't think I have the right to any of the Latinidade that's so important to them."

It's so difficult to admit that. Mom squeezes my hand with a worried look. "Nobody's ever said that, Nati. It's in your head, baby. Everybody loves you and misses you."

I try to swallow the rock that's stuck in my throat.

My hands are cold against hers.

"My cousins think that. That's why they refuse to speak English with me."

She shakes her head. "They want you to talk in Portuguese with them so you practice your native language. Remember your prima Renata? She moved to Uruguay for work and now she struggles with Portuguese, keeps getting it confused with Spanish. Everyone does the same to her. It's not to make your life hard."

I want to tell her that I don't buy it.

I want to tell her that she's wrong.

But everybody knows you can't just tell a Brazilian mom that she's wrong.

"You remember your primo Caio, don't you?" She tries, squeezing my hands again. I nod. He's maybe ten years older than me, ridiculously cute. I used to have a harmless crush on him as a kid. "You know he has a five-year-old, right?"

"Yeah. She's adorable."

"Little Vera is in love with you. She listens to all your songs, talks about you in school, about how you're her famous tia."

I breathe out as slowly as I can, as if it will somehow clean my mind of all these thoughts that I don't like.

It doesn't work. They're all still with me when I give Mom a staged smile and announce, feigning confidence, "I'll call Vovó later today. I promise."

Mom finally lets go of my hands. She knows me well, but not well enough to get past the smile that's designed for the cameras. Or maybe she does know and is choosing her battles again.

"Good. That will make me happy." As she sighs again, more deliberately this time, she glances around, and her eyes pause on my laptop, still open from last night. "Oh, you fell asleep watching something? What was it?"

"Um," I start, biting the insides of my cheeks. "It's a, um, it's a *Romeo and Juliet* retelling. But very, very different. Like, it was a heist movie, too. Weird. In a good way, I think? But weird. It's very darkly shot, and the leads are . . . well, Juliet didn't convince me much. But Romeo was . . ." I trail off.

Mom raises her eyebrows, encouraging me to continue. "He was okay." I shrug.

"All right. I'm sorry the movie wasn't what you were expecting." She gets up from my bed, and I don't feel like correcting her. "Don't forget to call Vovó." She winks. "Going to work now. Tchau, filha." She blows me a kiss.

I blow her a kiss back.

And then I'm alone in my room, groaning to myself, trying to gather the courage to either call my grandmother or close the movie tab from my computer.

I grab my pillow, bury my face in it, and scream at the top of my lungs.

It's three in the afternoon, and I have had my guitar on my lap for what feels like the past six hours, even if realistically it was probably one. I cross out all the lyrics I've written on the notepad next to me on the bed. I hate it, I hate it, I hate it.

Times like these I really wish we had a puppy or a kitten. A cute distraction.

Instead I'm doing my best to pretend I'm still working, even if nothing's coming.

I set my guitar aside and grab my phone. I go straight to my emails, and check that everything is all set for the superhero movie premiere on Saturday. My dress is ready for pickup. The hair and makeup artist will be waiting for me at a nearby hotel. I technically have a date for it, as I'm pretty sure William's schedule is clear. It'll be our big we're-a-couple moment, since we'll be together on the red carpet for the first time.

I put my phone down and stream the first notes of the theme song I wrote for the superhero movie. I recorded it so long ago I barely remember the lyrics.

I wrote "The Outsider" in Paris last year, after an event where I was supposed to mingle, but ended up only feeling self-conscious of how alone I was. This was before I met Trent. The song talks about feeling inadequate. Technically it's about the hero's powers overpowering him instead, his search for justice alienating him from his real life.

But whatever. Art can be interpreted in more ways than one.

I open my phone and text Brenda:

NATALIE:

can't write anything new

i'm freaking out

BRENDA:

have you considered writing about the

existential dread

and i mean DREAD

that applying to college brings?

NATALIE:

fdosighshi how can i help you?

BRENDA:

stop procrastinating

go write

I grab my guitar for emotional support and send another text, to a different person.

NATALIE:

so apparently i'm supposed to write new

songs

I keep staring at the screen until I can see the little dots that show he's writing. I suck my bottom lip and watch the screen intently until a message appears.

BRITISH BOYFRIEND:

You could always release an album of covers.

Sex Pistols, maybe?

I'm sure there'd be a public for that. ;)

I laugh, putting my guitar aside, and hug my legs.

NATALIE:

or i could suck it up

and make a new song

BRITISH BOYFRIEND:

That's a possibility too, of course. If you're into that.

Why can't you write? What's troubling you, mate?

I frown at the screen. *Mate?* Okay, then. I guess we're buddies now. Pals. Bros.

NATALIE:

it's my grandma's birthday today

i mean, i haven't been able to write

anything new in a while

but i think i was tired from the tour

and my life's been total chaos since . . .

what happened

i'm in a slump

and

i'm afraid of calling her too

I stare at the phone, waiting for a response. But the little dots never appear.

When my phone vibrates instead I nearly throw it away from me with the surprise. He's a *caller*. How could I possibly forget? Frowning, I slide right to answer his call and put the phone to my ear.

"Hello?"

"Why are you afraid of calling your grandma?"

"I guess . . ." I sigh. Okay, so we're doing this. "There's a lot there. And I don't know how to talk to her. I don't know if I am what she wants me to be. And that kind of scares me a bit. I'm lucky enough that I know Mom loves me unconditionally. But I'm an only kid. Grandma has so many options of grandkids she can love."

"Ah yes, as it is common sense that only parents with one child will love all their kids." He pauses. "I'm sure your grandma loves you. Like she must love all her grandkids."

I roll my eyes. "Yeah, but it's different. They're there with her. I'm . . . here."

He's quiet on the other end for a minute. I think he's

going to lecture me or maybe insist that she must love me very, very, very much. Instead, he asks, "Do you miss Brazil? Do you miss your family?"

I don't know how to answer that.

I look down, then close my eyes.

William hums in acknowledgment. "It's hard. I get that. I'm on the phone every day with Mum and my sisters, but I still miss them. I don't have anyone here in the States other than Cedrick, and that's . . . not the same. Do you think talking to her could make that feeling change?"

Eyes still closed, I feel some type of comfort falling over me. I don't know if it's the acceptance that I'm going to call my grandma, or if it's the softness of his words. Either way I find myself saying, "Maybe. But I'd like to find out."

"Brilliant!" he says, a bit too excitedly. "Let me know how the call goes. Bye!"

And then he hangs up.

I take the phone away from my ear and stare at the screen until it goes dark again. I can't believe he expects me to call her right now. But, at the same time, that was absolutely to be expected.

I Google the time zone differences, and then . . .

I take a deep breath and take the plunge.

When she doesn't answer on the first or the second ring, I tell myself that it's okay, and I should probably end the call now. She won't answer, and it won't be my fault that we don't talk today.

But on the third ring, she picks up, and my heart starts beating fast.

"Alô?" she asks.

I gather all my courage—and Portuguese—to reply, "Alô. Natalie aqui—" I shake my head, correcting myself, "Natalia. É a Natalia."

"Nati, meu amor!" she exclaims on the other side, so loud that I'm sure the majority of my family will now know that I called.

The way she says both things, both my childhood nickname with the Brazilian accent and all—*Nah-tchy*—and calling me meu amor, my love. It makes my eyes tear up, and I don't know why.

"Miss you, Vovó." I hold my breath. "Saudades."

Grandma chuckles, then says something I don't quite catch. I only know she's asking about Christmas. Natal. I don't respond right away, because if I'm honest, I still think it's for the best if I stay in Los Angeles this Christmas.

"Feliz aniversário," I tell her instead. "I hope you get a lot of love this year. You deserve it. Merece muito, minha vozinha."

I'm not sure how much she gets of what's English, but she starts making kissing noises on the other end. It makes me smile and cry at the same time. I want to hold the phone close to my heart, but instead I keep it very still next to my ear, as if a sudden movement could make the moment evaporate.

"Obrigada, filha! Obrigada!" she says.

"Te amo." I want to say I love you to the moon and back, though I don't know how to say that in Portuguese. I do know that moon is lua, but prepositions make it difficult to translate. Instead I say it again, "Te amo."

She says, "Te amo! I love you so much, so much." Her thick Brazilian accent, *I lovie yu sou muchie*, makes my heart so warm. I think she's crying, too.

"Okay. I have to go now, Vovó. Tenho que . . . irmos?"

"Tenho que ir," she corrects me. "Okay, filha. Vai. Nos falamos em breve? Talk soon?"

"Sim," I say. I suppose we could.

When we do hang up, I bring my phone to my chest. And before the adrenaline wears down, I'm already calling William to tell him about it.

Chapter 11

Mostly Harmless

he driver is Sean, the same one who had picked me up for my picnic date with William. We've been talking about superheroes for the last ten minutes with the partition down, and when he suggests that the most important hero is a guy I've never heard of, I say, "Now it will sound bad if I say I don't know who you're talking about."

He slaps his hand against the steering wheel with laughter. "I won't go to the tabloids to say that you don't know comic book superheroes, Miss Natalie, but you have to promise me you'll check out his movie."

"Deal, Sean."

He looks at me in the rearview mirror and then asks, "Are you nervous about the premiere?"

Writing a theme song for a blockbuster superhero

movie? Piece of cake compared to the anxiety about facing my first red carpet after Trent dumped me.

But I'm more nervous about where we're headed first, picking up William. I clear my throat and start to talk, then stop myself. Sean gives me another look through the rearview mirror, and I go with "Yes, a bit. It's a big night."

I'm glad that I'm not performing tonight, because I'd be in no way prepared. I'm hardly prepared to be photographed as it is. This is my first time being *around important people* since the People's Choice Awards event. Since my disgrace.

"I have a son who likes your music," he says out of nowhere, and when I don't immediately respond, he explains, "I know the tabloids have been giving you a hard time. But if you can make him dance, you're all right in my book."

While that's not enough to make my leg stop going up and down, warmth spreads through my chest. "That's . . . thank you so much. How old is he? What's his name?"

Sean starts telling me everything about his son and my nerves ease. I ask question after question about the boy, and I'm almost completely able to ignore the gift wrapped in silver on my left.

I've been preparing for tonight all day. My stylist, Erin, arrived at the crack of dawn to deliver my look for the evening. A perfectly tailored top that wraps around my neck fitting snugly over my breasts, finishing an inch above my belly button. With a thin strap around the back, the drama is in leaving most of my back exposed. A perfect long dark red skirt falls to my shoes, silver platform heels that make me four inches taller but still able to walk properly. My hair is up in a very high ponytail that cascades down my back, straight and silky. Long Swarovski earrings are exposed like a shower of crystals. A perfect tiny Salvatore Ferragamo black purse with a golden chain strap adorns my wrist.

Perfect, perfect, perfect.

When we arrive at William's hotel, my heart won't stop beating like it wants to break free from my rib cage. William's already waiting downstairs, in a beautifully tailored suit to go with his styled hair. He's not wearing a tie, but his crisp white shirt looks good against the navy of his suit. His hair is combed back and staying there, so his curls don't seem wild, only charming.

He's not wearing socks.

It happens to work with the outfit.

With an expression that's hard to read, he comes to the car. Sean opens the door for William, and after William spends a moment greeting him, he slides into the back of the limo and sits across from me.

Sean rolls up the partition without saying anything.

"Hi," William says.

"Hi," I respond slowly. I want to say that he looks gorgeous, but he doesn't seem ready for compliments. "Are you all right? You seem . . . off."

William rubs his hands together, then breathes in and out real loudly.

He's acting so weird.

"No, it's fine. Nothing much. Had a bit of a meeting with Ashley, but it's—it's okay."

I blink slowly. My Ashley? I suppose my Ashley is also his Ashley.

"What did she say?"

William glances around, as if Sean could possibly rat him out to Ashley.

"William," I press. "What did she say?"

"Just . . . ," he starts, then pauses, staring down at his shoes. They're an excellent pair of black oxfords. "She really has a problem with my socks. Did you know that? She hates my socks."

That startles a laugh out of me. "They are . . . fun."

He raises both of his eyebrows at me. "Brilliant, so you also hate my socks."

"I didn't say that. I'm just saying I guess I could see where she's coming from. Her job is to pick apart your image and predict your audience's reaction. Don't take it personally. She wants you to sell more."

I'm not entirely sure what would've been the right thing to say. But this wasn't it.

William stares at me as if he's seeing me for the first time.

I really don't like it.

His words are emphatic, an earnest look in his face. "I'm not a product to be sold." And then, in a nearly accusative tone, "Neither are you."

"Well." I snort. "Once we become famous, it's part of the deal." I point at my hair. "You think I like straightening my hair every day? Wearing this much makeup? Actually, the makeup I do like—" I throw my hands up. "But that's not the point! The point is that I accept it as part of the package. Because it is what it is. We have to look a certain way. *I* have to look a certain way."

He rests his elbows on his knees, surveying me.

I hate that he's so damn *gorgeous* in this suit and with his hair like this, because it makes it difficult to focus.

"Are you sure about that? Or are you molding yourself into something you *think* is more profitable?" Before I even have the chance to reply to that, he asks, "Are you happy changing who you are for fame?"

And maybe he doesn't know the right thing to say, either, but that? *Definitely* wasn't it.

I cross my arms like a shield across my chest.

"Listen, fame is a big deal. It's only through fame that I have the creative freedom to write my songs and do what I love. If you look down on fame, this is clearly the wrong business for you." I tilt my chin up. "Nobody makes it in Hollywood with *art*. But once we make it in Hollywood, we *get* to make art."

This time, William's at a complete loss for words.

He opens and closes his mouth, then seems to decide that this isn't worth it. Shaking his head, he sits back and turns to the dark window.

I can hear him murmur, "Remember why you're doing this," to himself, but I pretend I don't.

Neither one of us speaks for the remaining mortifyingly long half-hour car ride. When he isn't looking, I shove the small silver box in my purse.

The lights of the premiere event are blinding. I should have brought my inhaler.

Walking the red carpet is like being bathed in hot lights and still trying to look your best, promising your body a good shower later if it refuses to sweat under the spotlights.

We wait in silence for our turn.

William puts his hand on the small of my back and a shiver runs up my spine. I shift, which he must read as discomfort, because he immediately withdraws his hand. Instead he leans a little closer to my ear and asks, "Should I hold your purse or something?"

I notice his immense confusion.

I'm suddenly not nervous. But he's definitely nervous. Looking great, but lost.

"No, it's okay."

We try to beam at each other, but we've known each

other for a bit longer than these cameras have known *us*. I can tell he's faking it. He can probably tell I'm faking it, too. But the hostess gestures for us to move onto the red carpet next, so it's time to pretend.

Between smiling teeth, I say, "Put your arm around my waist."

William does. Then he whispers, "I thought you didn't want me to."

I choose to ignore that.

We walk side by side right into the hurricane that is the public eye—the cameras, the photographers, the reporters.

We put on a show, and we shine bright.

One of the reporters yells, "Are you really done with Trent Nicholson, Natalie?"

Another yells, "Natalie, can you tell us about your freak-out at the People's Choice Awards?"

A third yells, "Is this a rebound or is he for real?"

I politely smile at all of them, and then turn to face William. I move my hands to his biceps. He holds me back, like he isn't sure what he's supposed to be doing. His forehead has a touch of sheen. He's not used to the heat under the lights, and I feel like I failed him somehow, like I should've told him.

"I'm going to kiss you," I whisper. "Okay?"

Another reporter yells, "Is the song you wrote for the movie about Nicholson?"

And then William gets it. Or just decides to play the part no matter what.

"Okay," he whispers.

I close my eyes and the distance between us. He meets me halfway, one hand sliding up to the middle of my back, and I feel the shiver again, as the warmth of his body presses against me.

His lips cover mine, soft and warm, and my whole body goes hot.

I want to part my lips, but that would ruin the makeup. Instead I cup the side of his face, sliding my fingers to the back of his neck, finding warmth in his curls.

His firm hand on my back holds me closer, and I melt in his arms.

Then he moves away.

We stare at each other for a moment. I try to decode the look in his eyes, feeling a little self-conscious of how my face is probably flustered.

But the cameras go wild.

For a moment there, the stars are too small for us. We're gods.

I pull away properly and turn back to the cameras with a smile. We have to keep moving.

William eyes me seriously before smiling his slightly crooked super-white smile.

An *Entertainment Tonight* reporter comes at us with his

camera operator, who's staring at me like he wants to eat me alive. I clear my throat and turn to the reporter instead, a man who must be in his twenties but is playing older, with stubble and a tight bun.

"The hottest couple of the hour, oh my God!" the reporter shouts.

I offer him my Miss Pop Star attitude. William is frozen. I subtly poke him.

"Our goddess, Natalie!" He talks directly into the camera now, "Like Beyoncé or Madonna, only the greatest go by their first name!" He winks, then turns back to me. "So who are you wearing, love?"

The operator looks me up and down. I don't like where the camera seems to linger. I notice William clearing his throat, ready to interrupt, but even though I appreciate it, I don't let him.

"This is a Christian Dior exclusive, made specially for the occasion." I turn around for the camera, and as the reporter swoons, I add, "I love this shimmer." The reporter cheers.

"And you, William Ainsley, Hollywood's newest babe! Who are you wearing?"

The camera closes on William. *Make an effort*, I want to say.

He shoots me a glance like he wants to kill me for dragging him into this.

Doesn't he want Hollywood? This is Hollywood.

Then he flashes a charming smile. "All Armani. Don't know about the Hollywood part yet, though I hope I can star in some films here soon. Love the weather."

The reporter laughs. "Because London's so rainy! Yes! Love it!"

William offers him another smile, smaller this time.

The reporter winks at him, then yells at one of the actors passing us. "Oh my God, my favorite Chris! You have to tell us about your new movie." And off they go.

I breathe out my relief, and William tucks his hands into the pockets of his pants.

Again, I want to tell him that he's gorgeous in this suit, but again, it's definitely not the time. "Thanks for playing along."

He raises his eyes to me, scratches the back of his head. "Doing what?"

"Playing nice with the reporter." I shift around. "Kissing me."

William nods, not a hint of playfulness there.

I'm starting to feel sick.

"Now we watch the first screening. You must like superhero movies. Everybody does." I shrug.

He looks around, not scanning the crowd for famous faces, but apparently just to have somewhere to look at that isn't me. "Yeah, yeah. Superhero films are all right."

I bite the insides of my cheeks. "That wasn't so bad, was it?"

"Mostly harmless," he says. He's got a fake smile showing no teeth, and I realize now that the makeup team has hidden the birthmark on his cheekbone. I feel sadness tug inside me. "Let's go to the theater then, yeah?"

I nod. He offers his hand, and I take it.

We walk to the theater with cold hands that don't quite fit together.

Chapter 12

She Isn't Alone

The movie is as high octane as you'd expect a super-hero blockbuster to be. It's also shot brilliantly and has so many amazing stars that it's difficult to look away. Ten minutes in, I glance at William beside me, and his eyes are glued to the screen, absolutely transfixed by the experience.

Okay, so we started off on the wrong foot. We both said some unpleasant things. But it's not hopeless, right?

When "The Outsider"—*my* song—plays, William turns, and I can see some pride there. Hidden behind that scowl, which disappears the moment I stick my tongue out at him.

"C'mere," he says.

And then he offers me his arm.

Obviously he's doing it because we're out in public. But I do come closer. I rest my head on his shoulder, and we keep watching the movie.

It feels good to sit like that with him, and I can smell his cologne. Is that Clive Christian? Rose d'Arabie? I'm possibly leaning too close, because he turns to me with a slight frown.

With a hand on my shoulder, he murmurs, "Everything all right?"

Sure. Just smelling you.

I take a deep breath and glance around. Everyone's paying attention to the movie, so maybe . . . maybe it's all right. I open my purse and hand him the silver box, putting some distance between us.

I don't explain because, honestly, I'm not sure what to say.

William shoots me a curious look before doing his utmost not to make any noise as he opens the gift. When he finds the superhero socks inside, the corner of his mouth quirks up.

"For me?" he asks quietly.

I roll my eyes. "No, just having you hold on to these for a bit."

He laughs, holding them close to his chest. "I love them."

We smile at each other. For the first time all night, it seems genuine.

I am way too comfortable entering this party with William.

It's not that I don't *want* to feel comfortable around him; I'm surprised at how natural it is. Squeezing his hand as we make our way into the room, I'm glad I'm not attending this party alone, but more than that, I'm at ease with him. I like how his warm hand feels in mine.

It's great . . . for a fake boyfriend and all.

"Thoughts on the movie?" I ask, my voice loud enough to be heard above the chatter and music. He gives me a lopsided grin, and before he can start, I warn, "You can't say that you're waiting for the sequel to form an opinion."

"That's exactly what I was going to say!" He laughs.

"I know. That open ending . . ." I make a face. "But for real, did you like it?"

I hope he'll say yes. I hope he'll say that it doesn't matter that we argued in the car. I hope he'll say that the second he heard my song he understood.

Before any of that can happen, we're interrupted. Valentina Fiore, a former model who's been designing her own fashion line the past few years, approaches us in a neon-pink dress and a smirk.

"Oh my God! Hi, Natalie!"

She hugs me, and William lets me go. "Valentina, hi!" I put some distance between us, smiling my biggest smile to match hers. "Look at how pretty you are in pink!"

"Queen, you're the prettiest! Ah, reina!" she says, with an exaggerated accent that I suppose is meant to sound Mexican. "Who's the hottie?" She comes closer and touches William's chest.

Full-on touches his chest with both hands.

He takes a step back, and I can tell he's trying to mask his shock, but he doesn't do a very good job. "This hottie is called William," he says as he takes her hands and politely removes them from his chest. "He is also taken, sorrowfully."

In the split second it takes her to stand back, a thousand thoughts run through my mind. First, I'm indignant that she's taken the liberty to touch him like that. I want to step in and tell her to back off. That she wouldn't like it if a man did that to her.

Then his words sink in.

He's taken.

Warmth spreads over my chest and face, and I bite back a smile.

"'Sorrowfully,'" Valentina imitates him, then turns to me again. "He's British, how cute!"

I raise my eyebrows and wait for her to go.

She eventually does.

"What was that?" he asks, but I have a feeling it's more to himself than me.

I raise my shoulders. "She keeps calling me reina. I don't think she realizes I don't speak a word of Spanish. Maybe she thinks I'm Hispanic? Maybe she thinks all Latinas are Hispanic?" I frown, talking more to myself than to him.

His eyes dance as I speak. A waiter passes by with smoked salmon cannoli, and I take one for me. William does the same.

"It's kind of cute when you do that."

I snap my head in his direction, blinking slowly. "Do what? Cute? What?"

William smiles. "Your monologues. They're cute."

His eyes look darker somehow, almost brown. Do they always change color?

But William looks over, and I follow his gaze.

Behind him, three people are watching us. Two I don't know, but one of them is a photographer from one of the biggest tabloids in Los Angeles. No camera in sight, but he's still paying attention.

Maybe that's it. He spotted them, too. He's a good actor, I'll give him that.

I clear my throat. "There's a lot of actors here. Do you want me to introduce you? Networking done right." I wink. Then I kick myself—have I become a winker?

William does that thing where he shifts his weight to the other foot. "I don't know. Maybe later?"

I don't understand his hesitation, but I nod. "Whenever you're ready, I guess."

That's when I spot my producer talking to the director of the movie. Aline Hernandez, who produced my theme song as well as quite a few from my last album, wears her hair up in a braided bun, with dramatic orange eyeshadow. Nina Kim, the director of the movie, wears a tail dress with a deep V-neck. They're fierce and fabulous and so tall in their five-inch heels, posing even when they're just talking to each other.

My face lights up looking at them.

"Oh my God. I haven't been introduced to Nina Kim yet. And she's with Aline! She produced 'The Outsider.'" I press my lips together, trying to contain my excitement. William follows my eyes to the women, then back at me.

"You want to say hello, don't you?" he teases. I nod. He takes my hand in his and says, "So let's do it. Maybe it won't hurt if I start meeting directors." He adds the second part with a frown, but I appreciate his hand in mine.

We start toward them, but we don't make it very far.

Whispers seem to fill the space around me, and I notice a few people's gazes bouncing from me to someone behind me. I turn around, and sure enough, there's Trent, wearing a basic black suit, his blond hair perfectly tousled, and his big blue eyes narrowed on us.

And now that he knows that I've spotted him, he's walking in our direction.

Chapter 13

It Should Have Been Me

This party was supposed to be William and my official couple debut. It was supposed to be a night to make connections and network, hopefully introduce William around, and just have a good time with my friend.

Because we are friends. Or something.

But watching Trent come closer, I know that this party is headed for disaster.

Faster than Trent can make his way to us, I make our way out. I grab William's hand, saying over my shoulder, "Let's go meet Aline and Nina Kim!" and drag him across the room. All my excitement about meeting the director has turned into desperation to get out of this situation as fast as possible.

"Aline, hi! This is my boyfriend, William Ainsley!" I

announce, flustered. When the two women turn in our direction, they both frown. Aline's frown quickly turns into a smile, though. "He's an actor," I add, as if that would make my approach smoother.

William stops by my side, eyes wide and staring at me like I've grown a second head. I turn to Nina Kim.

"Nina, I am so happy to finally meet you! It was such a pleasure to work on the soundtrack of this movie."

Recognition dawns and Nina greets us. She shakes hands with me and William. "We all loved the song the minute we listened to it. It really captures the hero's inner battle." She pauses, turning to William. "It's a pity we weren't aware of you before. Cory Bailey did a fantastic job, but you seem like you would have made a great Wade as well."

Wade, the superhero's witty best friend, had enough screen time that I'm sure he'll have a fan club as soon as the movie comes out. Maybe he already does, based on the trailers alone.

It's a nice thing to hear. Unfortunately, William's still gaping at me. I tug at his jacket and incline my head toward Nina, hoping he'll get the message to pay attention.

"Pardon me, Ms. Kim, I didn't quite catch that."

As she repeats it, Aline touches my arm. I lean closer, and she whispers, "Is there a reason Trent Nicholson is standing a few feet behind you like he's a fan waiting in line for his turn?"

Aline seems almost proud. Her eyes flick between

Trent and me. I pause awkwardly. Aline and I aren't really close. She's a genius producer with whom I work well, not a friend. I learned at fifteen that I can't confide in coworkers after the whole world found out who I had a crush on, all because of a chatty sound engineer.

I shrug and turn to Nina and William, trying to catch up on their conversation—they're definitely getting along, which is *good*. I want to be happy for them and not terrified of what happens when the conversation finishes.

"Natalie, can I talk to you for a sec?"

We all stop and turn to Trent, who apparently got tired of waiting and is interrupting with his typical Hollywood megawatt smile.

To be fair, probably neither Aline nor Nina cares that much about my past with Trent. If Nina didn't once talk about pulling the song from the soundtrack because of what happened at the People's Choice Awards, I'm sure it doesn't really matter to her that he's here now. But the way William looks at me, a question on his face, tells me that he does. He cares.

What am I supposed to do?

I swallow the knot in my throat and put on my default camera smile, because that's what I'm hardwired to do.

"Cool," he says, taking my arm and pulling me away.

I don't look behind to check whether William's okay. I know that he's talking to one of Hollywood's greatest directors. He's in good hands. He's networking.

When I yank my arm from Trent, we're already a few feet away. A waiter passes us and Trent grabs a glass of champagne. After a gulp, he says, "I saw your little kiss on the red carpet." He cocks an eyebrow at me. "You know that should have been me, right?"

My brows furrow. "What—what are you talking about?"

He stands tall, chin up, and takes another sip. "I know you kissed him like that to make me jealous."

My hands are shaking slightly.

"My God. Have you always been this infuriating?"

Trent laughs. "Your new boyfriend isn't infuriating at all though, is he? He's so weak . . . like his follower count. Embarrassing." He snorts.

He doesn't care about me. He doesn't care about what I've been through. He never even asked me how I'm doing. You know who did, the first time we talked after the fiasco? William. William, who has been kind to me from day one.

Trent only wanted me because he thought it would boost his career.

Or maybe he never cared, because he's not *capable* of caring.

It all boils up inside me, but then I see the photographer watching us from afar, far enough that it's not *too* suspicious, but close enough that he'll be there if I break down and do something dramatic.

I've learned my lesson in that department.

I take a deep breath, counting to ten in my head as I put into place my most plastic smile.

"I don't want to hear from you again, okay?"

Also in place? Trent's smirk. He seems to think that I'm joking, because he tilts his head to the side and says, "Ooookay."

Does he think that's charming? Was it ever?

I leave him standing there and head back to William.

I'm clutching my purse so hard that my knuckles hurt.

I suddenly hate these lo-fi beats. I want music I can scream to.

Aline isn't there anymore, but Nina and William are still talking. When I approach them, William stops mid-sentence, eyes paused on me with a question that I can't answer easily. I nod at Nina Kim.

She glances between us and excuses herself. "It was really nice to meet you both. I'll be in touch."

Once we're alone, I want to fall into his arms and get the longest hug in the world. But when he turns to me, he doesn't look very huggable. He looks pissed.

"I can't believe you bailed on me," he accuses.

My lips part, and I take a step back. "I *what*?"

William sighs, like this is so tiring. Like I'm so tiring. "First you drag me over here without any warning, and then you bail on me. You left me here to make conversation with strangers."

I snort. "We were heading over here anyway. What are you talking about?"

But I know what he's talking about. And he knows that I know it, too.

Is he upset that everyone saw me talking to my ex? Is he worried about how that will affect the way people perceive us? Does he genuinely care what Trent and I talked about?

"Everything about this is . . ." He trails off and shakes his head. "Everyone pretending to like one another . . . It's so . . ."

I want to press: *What. What. What?!*

Instead, I let my anger rise up and step into his personal space. "Aw, no. You're too good for celebrity culture? Valentina annoyed you, and having to make conversation with Nina annoyed you. Even though she's brilliant. That's what you wanted to say in the car anyway. That you're too good for this." And somehow, I make *this* sound like *me*.

William stares at me.

I hate that he looks hurt. He doesn't have the right to look hurt.

I am hurt.

"I don't think you need this, Natalie."

He sounds soft. He sounds genuine. He sounds like he doesn't want to fight.

But he's got nothing on my anger and frustration.

"You don't know what I need." I scoff. "You're the stage boyfriend, remember?" He grimaces, but I'm not done. *She,* the eight-year-old me, is not done. "And you're doing it for the fame, too, so one hell of a hypocrite you are."

He doesn't move.

"I'm not doing it for fame. I'm doing it for the money."

It's like a sucker punch. I snort, shaking my head.

"That's so much worse."

With that, I walk away.

Chapter 14

*

JK

"You look gloomy," Brenda says, pointing her ice cream spoon at me.

I raise my shoulders and steal the spoon from her, diving into the bowl of ice cream. It's homemade. Brenda's sister is the best. "The premiere didn't exactly go the way I expected. Now I have Trent texting me that he wants me back, which is *weird*, since I know he's still with Reese, and I haven't talked to William in, like, a week."

Brenda throws her feet on top of my lap. "I'm sorry the paparazzi caught you leaving in separate cars. Bobbi must've been angry."

I stare at her feet on my lap. "She had questions. I hate that the tabloids are speculating about our *rocky relationship*. It's not rocky. Everything is perfectly all right. We haven't talked in a week, but that's all right. Perfectly all right."

Brenda steals the spoon back and hooks an arm around the bowl. "Well, you guys haven't had any important events or anything this week. Why would you have talked to him?"

I start to respond, but I'm interrupted by an annoying sound of construction. "What's happening upstairs?"

"Dad wants to prove that he's a functional husband by being heteronormative and building Mom a closet or something? Being the man of the house?" She rolls her eyes, and takes another spoonful of ice cream. "You're so lucky you live in a fancy apartment and not in a house."

I cock an eyebrow. "Uh, my mom's an architect. The fact that we live in an apartment doesn't stop her from going wild with renovations every summer. Our home is the perfect pet project that she goes back to whenever she's not challenged enough at work." That makes Brenda laugh. "You think I'm joking, but I'm not."

"C'mon. She's great. Your apartment looks like it came out of one of those renovation TV shows." I'm about to start arguing when she adds, "Any version of your apartment."

"I think I'd rather live in a house, but Mom likes the building because it's so safe, so we don't need to hire security people. She said the only way I was staying in a house alone while she was off at work would be with dozens of suited up people guarding the house, and I'm not up for that."

I think Brenda misses the last of what I say, because her dad starts drilling the wall, and the second I stop talking, he seems to drop something heavy, and we both jump. We share a look, and I'm about to ask if he's okay, when she announces, "I don't ask about what's going on up there, and they don't ask me about college applications. It's a perfect system."

I narrow my eyes. "How's that going, by the way? Have you started, or . . . ?"

Brenda throws her head back against the arm of the couch and makes a whale noise. "Yes, Mom, I have. *Anyway.* Let's go back to your terrible week."

I shake my head. "No, let's not. I know—well, I *imagine* how stressful college applications can be. . . . Best thing about graduating high school on tour and not thinking about this again. But what's going on, anyway? What's really up?"

Brenda rolls her eyes, combing her thick brown hair through her fingers. She looks mad at me for even asking, but eventually I win our staring contest, and she shrugs. "It's kind of bizarre, all right? Deciding on a four-year plan when neither my best friend nor my girlfriend can commit to *anything* long-term at the moment."

I press my lips together, my mind racing for something to say. She shakes her head again, raising her index finger.

"Don't. It's fine. I knew what I was signing up for when I stuck around for you, and when I started dating an international DJ. Padma's time is split between Los Angeles with her family and me and the rest of the world with her job. You've got your own things, too. It's just . . ." She gestures dismissively.

But it matters to me. I pull her into a hug, and she hugs me back, sighing heavily. "I want to be brilliant like you two. But what if I can't even get into college?"

"You're brilliant," I say, then kiss the top of her head. "You're perfect because you're you."

Brenda squeezes the life out of me, then takes a deep breath. She smiles softly as she falls back on the couch. "Trent's a loser for letting you go." She rests her feet on my lap again, and I push them away, but when she insists, I relent. At least her feet are warm. "He's always been a loser, actually. I told you that when I first met him."

"You did make your opinion perfectly clear, yes." I grimace, then laugh. "I know you're right. I guess I thought . . . I guess I thought I needed him. And no, I don't think I miss him. But I miss what he represented. I sort of felt . . . like I'd made it. Because I was dating the American knight in shining armor."

Brenda makes a face. "The US isn't doing very great, is it?"

I chuckle, playing with the ends of her jeans to distract myself. "He said that William is *weak*." I raise my eyes to meet Brenda's. "Like, how dare he? That's such a ridiculous thing to say."

"Yeah, no doubt. Like saying that William's not hot and fierce, but soft, like that's a bad thing to start with. That's also pretty crappy." She grins when I flip her off. "I said he was cute when I first saw his picture. And I know this thing is for show, but you guys seem to have become friends, so why not treat him like one?"

"Yeah, that'd be cool, but we're not speaking. We had a fight."

Brenda does something that resembles a growl. I can't really tell.

All I know is she puts aside the bowl of ice cream and jumps on top of me, shaking me by the shoulders so hard that I have to slap her away from me. "Get off!"

She does get off—more like she falls to the side—but she seems to feel the need to show her annoyance in more ways than one, so she punches me in the shoulder. I grab my arm and scowl at her.

"You're such a mess, Natalie." She rolls her eyes. "You two had a fight, big deal! If you'd given up on me the first fight we had, I'd have haunted you for the rest of your life, because I'd see you become famous and get all that free stuff, and I'd know in my heart that I could have been your groupie."

I bite back a smile. "You'd haunt me? Does that mean you'd be dead?"

"Possibly. Butterfly effect and all." She picks up the bowl of ice cream again. "You don't know what would happen. But I know that if you keep whining about how you two had a fight and don't do anything to fix it, then you're being weird."

"Weird," I repeat, looking at her.

"Weird. People fight. Boo-hoo. What's with being so pressed about it?"

She doesn't know the details, of course. She doesn't know the words we said.

She doesn't know that he's doing it for the money.

She doesn't know that he thinks he's better than me.

I sink a little on the couch.

She tries to stick her toe into my mouth. I slap her away, screaming, "Merda!" If she takes the hint, she doesn't seem to care. "Stop that, Jesus Christ!"

"Text him!" she commands.

I'm this close to punching her.

"Just a text. Ask him out to coffee or something so you guys can talk it out."

"You know what? Screw this. I'm going to text him."

Brenda cheers and does a ridiculous little dance on the couch. I'm not watching because my eyes are on my phone, sending him the stupid message:

> **NATALIE:**
>
> i know things are weird
>
> i don't want things to be weird
>
> coffee later today?
>
> i can buy you pie
>
> you can eat it all by yourself

"Done, I did it, now get off me," I tell her, but I'm still staring at the screen. She laughs and says something that I completely miss because I cut her off, saying, "Oh, he's replying, he's replying! The little dots!"

She jumps over to my side.

> **BRITISH BOYFRIEND:**
> Sorry, I'm booked.

I turn to Brenda. "What does that mean, *he's booked*? How could he possibly be booked? He's only been in LA for a few weeks—has it even been a month? How could—?"

"Shut up and see what he texted next." She pokes me.

I look down at the phone in my hands.

> **BRITISH BOYFRIEND:**
> Jk, jk.
> (That means 'just kidding', in case you
> were wondering.)
> (Not like, 'jurassic kicks', or something.
> Which would be an interesting movie
> concept.)
> (Dinosaurs who are also into football?)
> (Or should I say soccer?)
> (Hint: the whole world says football. Get
> with the program, Americans.)
> Anyway . . . sure. What time?

I look back at Brenda, biting the inside of my mouth.

She *giggles*. Like a schoolgirl. "He's such a dork!"

"Completely, yes."

She pokes my cheek and says, "Stop doing that. Everyone can tell you're nervous, and you're probably butchering the inside of your mouth."

I stop biting my cheeks.

And flip her off, of course, in time for her mom to see as she passes by the room.

We both freeze.

But Brenda's mom grins and comes closer to the couch. "Natalia, oi, bonita!" I grin, especially when she slaps Brenda's feet so they're back on the floor. "Have manners, Brenda!"

Brenda's face contorts in the panic only known to a Brazilian daughter who desperately wants to talk back to a Brazilian mom but knows it's not a good idea. Eventually, Brenda takes a deep breath and pointedly looks away, probably to avoid my knowing smirk.

"How's your mother?" Brenda's mom asks, like always, and then doesn't let me answer. "Has Brenda offered you some water? Some food? Ice cream isn't real food." She grabs the bowl, shaking her head. *"You need to treat your friend better,"* she says.

Brenda relaxes. "You know she only gets like that with you, right? My girlfriend is *just as famous as you* but because she's a DJ and not a pop star, Mom treats her like a commoner."

I do my best not to laugh, because Brenda's mom is glaring.

She points at Brenda. "You're impossible. Have you told your sister Natalia is here?"

"Yeah. She already came to collect her selfie," Brenda replies, then rests her head on my shoulder. "If I make my famous friend sleep over, am I off the hook with helping clean the mess Dad's creating upstairs?"

Brenda's mom looks from me to her, then shakes her head, walking to the kitchen and speaking so fast in Portuguese that I don't catch any of it. I poke Brenda's middle to communicate how unnecessary that was, and she yells like I've wounded her deeply.

We laugh, and when our laughter dies down, she announces, "You know Padma thinks that's weird?"

I frown. "That your mom thinks I'm the queen?"

"That we play-fight all the time." She shrugs. "I think it's because she's not Brazilian. She doesn't get that we're... touchy-feely about everything. So we get physical a lot." She huffs, head back on my shoulder.

I consider this.

I remember playing with my cousins, both boys and girls, when we were little, but the girls were always told to be less aggressive when we were children. To be sweet. I think that's why every Brazilian teenage girl I know has moments when they explode and just want to hit everything.

It's not like I can be like this with anyone but Brenda. If

the tabloids saw us play-fighting, there would probably be articles about how we have an abusive and toxic friendship.

Brenda shrugs again. "I don't think a lot about it. Aaaaanyway. Are you excited to meet your fake boyfriend and make things right again?"

The question catches me off guard, and I reply without a second thought, "Maybe a bit. Mostly nervous."

She smiles at me, like she knows something I don't, but she doesn't broach the subject again.

Chapter 15

A Major Favor

William and I meet in the same café we met in the first time, but this time we sit inside in a reserved booth. I come in with a cap and sunglasses, and only take them off when William walks through the door, in blue jeans and a ripped orange shirt with the sleeves rolled up. I immediately look down to his feet: he's wearing sneakers and black socks with pumpkins on them. Happy October.

I smile, setting my cap and sunglasses aside.

Will he think I look cute in this button-down dungaree maroon dress with a white long-sleeved shirt underneath? I run my hand over my hair, tilting my head to the side a little.

The first thing I say when he sits across from me on the booth is "There's always something ripped." I point at his shirt. When he looks down with a question mark on his face, I explain, "Because that day at the picnic you were wearing ripped jeans?"

William sighs softly and says, "Darling, *I'm* ripped."

That actually makes me snort, and he laughs, too.

Some of the ice between us melts.

"I asked for some lemonade, if that's okay." Before he can call me out for remembering his order, I tell him, "I am sorry about being . . . I'm sorry about that night. I shouldn't have said the things I said. I should've prepared you better for what the premiere would be like, and . . . I don't know. I feel like I said some harsh things." I start biting the insides of my cheeks, then stop. "You're my friend. I don't want you to think that I'm a self-obsessed, entitled diva."

He blushes and nods. "I'm sorry, too. I shouldn't have acted like I know what's best for you. Only you know what's best for you."

I raise my chin. "And also I'm your friend? Because I'm going to need some validation on that front. Artists are extremely needy and insecure, and it makes me very stressed out that you're not."

William offers me a proper smile. "We're friends, Natalie! We're friends."

I grin back at him. "Good." But I can't help adding, "Even if you're doing this for money, I'm glad that you're my fake boyfriend."

That gives him pause. The waiter comes by to set down our lemonades—I'm giving up my smoothie for this today—and then he tells me, "Yes. It is about the money. But it's not like that."

I put up my hand. "It's okay. You do you. You're allowed to like money."

He runs both of his hands through his hair. The messiness is endearing. I like it better than the suave look he had on the red carpet. It feels more *William*.

"How do I explain it? Well, I do like money, of course, who doesn't? But that's not why I decided to jump on a plane to the United States when my agent said he had a way for me to quickly make . . . a lot of dollars." William sits a little closer to the table and lowers his voice. I instinctively move closer, too. "I have five siblings. I'm the second oldest. My older sister, Amanda, and I, we both always took care of the family, but now that Dad's gone . . ."

I set my jaw, my stomach sinking.

William glances away to collect his feelings. "He left us so much debt. My side gigs and Amanda's accountant job aren't enough to help the whole family. There's too many of us."

I shut my eyes.

What the hell.

"There's a lot that's weird for me, that makes me . . . uncomfortable. My followers blowing up, people suddenly taking an interest in my family and following *them*, too. My little sister Lou had to delete all her social accounts because people were flooding them with questions about me," William says, his head down for a moment, trying to murder his cuticles. I can feel my cheeks flush with heat when he mentions Louise. "I don't really care about Hollywood, but I care about their big paychecks. I have no interest in becoming a celebrity, I don't. But I . . . I have to do right by my family."

My hand has a mind of its own, and it reaches out for his, stopping his little act of self-penitence with the cuticles. I squeeze his hand.

"I am so, so sorry, William. People shouldn't be doing that. Maybe I can—"

"It's not your fault," he adds quickly. "Ashley's assistant gave me a big check, and that's helping so much. If you want to take responsibility for anything, that's what you should be focusing on."

I reluctantly let go of his hand, shaking my head slowly. "I . . ." I trail off, and then look up at him again. "I'm so sorry that your family is going through this. But I'm also happy that they have you." I mean it, too. It's the most honest I've been in a while.

He looks at me again, his eyes welling up. He laughs about it, keeps his hand firm in mine, and with the other he wipes the tears out of his eyes. "I miss them, if I'm honest. It hasn't even been that long, and we FaceTime every day. My sister Louise sends me memes almost hourly. . . . But I miss them, yeah. It's hard being here on my own, in an unfamiliar industry and a foreign country and all."

It makes me admire him even more.

I am preparing myself to tell him that—that I think he's brave, that I think he's kind, that I think he's *beautiful*. But he doesn't give me the chance. Instead he changes the subject.

"So, um, your grandma. Have you talked to her again since you called her?"

The abrupt shift makes me laugh uncomfortably. "I mean, no, but that was, like, yesterday." I raise my shoulders, a little defensive. "It's complicated." And then, for no apparent reason, I tell him something I haven't told either of my closest friends: "Mom wants us to go back to Brazil for Christmas."

He nods. "My family's Jewish, and Hanukkah is important to us. Ashley said it was okay if I went home and stayed with them that week, that as long as the tabloids are being fed, et cetera, it's not a breach of contract?"

I wait for him to say something else, until I realize that he's waiting for my okay. I have to do my best not to laugh. Does he really think that I would hold the contract against him and be like, *you can't go?* "Yeah. Sure."

"Thanks," he says. "Are you excited about Christmas with your family?"

I glance around for a second. "I don't . . . have what you have with your family, William." I make a face, take a sip of the sweet lemonade so saying that out loud won't taste as bitter. "I love them. But from a distance. They think I'm a snob. They don't really like me."

"I think that you make a lot of assumptions about what people think of you."

I take the deepest of breaths, make a pillow of my arms, and rest my face in it.

He still sounds soft but firm when he asks, "What's really the problem?"

And the answer pours out of me before I can think twice. "I'm afraid." I raise my head from my arms and meet his gaze. "If I keep my distance, then they can't reject me. They can't hurt me. But if I go, then I'll have to know. I'll have to live it. I'll have to actually . . . be vulnerable."

Should I write about that? No, I shouldn't. It's not the first time I've thought about it, but it's the first time I've said it out loud. Hearing my own voice saying these words . . . I'm equal parts relieved and embarrassed. Embarrassed because I know I'm not supposed to feel that way. If I'm brave enough to step on a stage with hundreds of thousands of eyes on me, surely I shouldn't be afraid of my own family?

But relieved too, because it's no longer just my secret to keep.

He nods, taking another sip from his lemonade. "*Or* you could have a wonderful Christmas at home. With people who love you."

I tilt my head and consider that. Maybe.

My phone vibrates, and we exchange a look.

Oh God. What now?

Chapter 16

Shady

> **BOBBI:**
>
> I have amazing news.
>
> Let's schedule a meeting ASAP

I stare at my phone, feeling something in my stomach turn. I look up at William, and he's checking his own phone. "Something wrong?"

With a hint of suspicion, he shrugs. "I don't know. Cedrick texted me a while ago, but I hadn't seen. Says he wants to meet, that someone made an offer. I don't know what the project is, though."

"Aren't you supposed to audition for roles for that to happen?"

"Typically. But sometimes when they like your work,

they can make an offer to you first. And if you say no, then they open auditions." He pauses. "I have never gotten an offer like that before. That's . . . weird."

"You know what," I say, turning my phone screen down. "Let's just quit everything, and start over somewhere where nobody knows who we are, and nobody writes fanfic about us together."

I'm obviously joking, but his smirk makes me pause. "Fans have written about us together?" He raises his eyebrows. "Is it smutty?"

I roll my eyes and make a face at him.

"JK!" he yells, laughing. The actual letters. J and K. "Just kidding."

I'm about to tell him he doesn't have to explain the acronym, when I realize I don't care. His phone is forgotten on the other side of the table. We're going to have these lemonades and then we're going to ask for some cheesecake, and I'll schedule a meeting with Bobbi when I'm home.

"You know," William starts. "I know we're only a month into the contract and everything . . . but if it's okay with you, I should go to London for the next few days. I need to help my family with the bank. Amanda's the only one who really knows how to handle these situations, but she's very overworked, so I need to help Mum."

"Oh." I fight the urge to reach out for his hand on the

table between us. "That's—don't worry about the contract. It's okay, really. I promise. Go to London." I offer him a small smile. "Family stuff sounds like the most important type of stuff."

He gives me an appreciative smile.

To myself, I think: *Stop talking about the contract.*

The idea was that Mom and I would watch a movie together, but I can't stop thinking about Bobbi's proposition that she pitched to me over a call earlier this evening. She seems to think it's such a golden opportunity, but . . . I'm not so sure.

I try to focus on the movie, but it's boring. My mind starts wandering, and before I know it, I'm sneaking a peek at Mom and unlocking my phone to check the time. She's so engrossed in the movie she doesn't seem to have noticed that I'm on my phone.

Biting the insides of my cheeks, I go to my texts and click on William's chat.

NATALIE:

DON'T CALL!!!!

i'm supposed to be paying attention to

a movie

BRITISH BOYFRIEND:

?

NATALIE:

i'm with mom

and you always end up calling

so like, now i can't answer the phone

i'm pretending to be a good daughter

BRITISH BOYFRIEND:

It's delightful that you're actually pointing

out that you're pretending.

NATALIE:

yes i . . . i am delightful

anyway

what did cedrick want?

was it shady?

BRITISH BOYFRIEND:

I wouldn't say it's shady.

But it's . . . I don't know how I feel about

this.

That director we talked with?

She really wants me to play a sidekick.

NATALIE:

THAT'S AMAZING

CONGRATULATIONS OMG

BRITISH BOYFRIEND:

Not so fast.

NATALIE:

if you say you wanted the hero or nothing

i'm going to leave mom and go straight to

your hotel

and kick your ass

BRITISH BOYFRIEND:

It's a four-movie contract with exclusivity.

I couldn't be in anything else.

NATALIE:

can they do that?????????

BRITISH BOYFRIEND:

Because I'm a no-name actor who'd be

getting my big break. . . .

Yeah, they can.

And I don't know what to do.

You?

What did your agent want?

NATALIE:

well, my thing was actually shady

you know how i've ALWAYS written all my
stuff?

some artists don't

but it's my BRAND

I ALWAYS WRITE MY STUFF

BRITISH BOYFRIEND:

Yes . . . ?

NATALIE:

bobbi found someone willing to sell a
whole album to me

and i'd take credit for the lyrics too

but i'd be singing someone else's truth

it's like my own agent gave up on me
writing my stuff

it hasn't even been that long but . . .

i can write songs. i'm just . . . not doing it
right now

BRITISH BOYFRIEND:

Oh.

NATALIE:

yeah.

oh.

hey

you don't want to make a decision now do

you?

because i don't

i'd very much like to not make a decision

at all

BRITISH BOYFRIEND:

I'm listening.

** reading

NATALIE:

you know my friend padma?

dj lotus?

she's headlining a new festival

BRITISH BOYFRIEND:

You never introduced me to any of your

friends.

Should I be concerned? Am I not a good

enough boyfriend?

NATALIE:

LISTEN!!!!!!

i mean, READ!!!!

let's go to this festival in portugal as soon

as you get back from London and forget about our wonderful but undoubtedly shady agents

BRITISH BOYFRIEND:

That's very out of nowhere.
I mean, I'd like to. But I don't know if I can.

NATALIE:

i'm paying

BRITISH BOYFRIEND:

It'll be my honor to escort you to this important event.

Chapter 17

I Know

"Are you okay? You look whiter than usual," I tell William.

William has been quiet since we got on the plane. Now he has a white-knuckle grip on the arms of his first-class seat. He nods briefly at me without looking away from the flight attendant, so I poke him.

When he turns to me with wide eyes, I ask, "Are you afraid of flying?"

He scoffs, shaking his head, but the death grip on the arms of his seat says otherwise. "Of course I'm not. I'm European. We travel around on low-cost flights all the time. It's how we're so cultured," he teases with a cocked eyebrow.

I roll my eyes. "This isn't a low-cost airline. Unlike your

usual flying bus, this probably won't catch fire while we're up in the air."

His nostrils flare and I see him swallow a knot.

"I don't—"

I slap his arm. "JK, William, JK!" When he gives me a horrified look, I clarify, "Just kidding. It means just kidding."

That does get a little smile out of him.

"You know, it's all right if you're not a big fan of flying. I'm not a big fan of cruises. I always get seasick. Ever been?"

His eyes go from me to the flight attendant, still giving safety instructions ahead of us. "I really think we should listen to him."

"Nah. It's always the same. Plus if the plane is going down, we're probably dying anyway." I poke his middle again, and he actually glares at me. I'm living for this. "Did you know that in all of history there's only been one actual commercial plane *crash* where there were survivors? Captain Scully in New York wasn't a crash, only a malfunction in the engines because of birds. But a crash . . . It was in Brazil, too. In the seventies."

William takes a deep breath. "Yeah? How did they survive?"

He probably wants a distraction, but I can't help but think about that time at the movie premiere when he told me that it was cute when I talk a lot. If my cheeks are blushing a bit now, that's simply not my fault.

"The pilot had to insert the coordinates to the destination—it wasn't automatic. So, let's say, instead of inserting 030, he put only 30. And the plane read it as 300 instead. Some passengers who were used to taking that flight tried warning the pilot, but he didn't want to admit that something was wrong . . . so eventually the fuel ran out, and he said to the passengers that they were going down: 'E eu desejo a todos um bom fim.'" I do my best impersonation of a Brazilian man, and he blinks at me. "It's from the black box. You can hear it on YouTube. He says: *And I wish you all a good ending.*"

His eyes widen, and his grip on the seat arms tightens. "He said that? He actually said that?"

I nod. "What softened the landing, *sort of,* was the trees. Very tall, lots of branches . . . when it did hit the ground, it wasn't as intense anymore, and most people were wearing seat belts. Still, some lived, and some didn't." I shrug. "Then they had to survive in the Amazon rain forest until one of the groups found a farmer and went back for the rest of them."

"Whoa," he says. He still has an ironclad grip on the armrest.

I laugh. "I can see that you're very chill."

That makes him break into a smile. "Oh, I'm extremely chill, darling." He winks.

I give him my most unimpressed look. "You only use

darling when you're full of it. The only appropriate response is to laugh at you."

"I choose to think you're laughing *with* me instead, mind you."

I ignore him, reaching for the screen in the seatback in front of him. "Mom's the one who drove me to the airport, you know. She had a flight the other day to Boston for work, and she told me they have good stuff to watch now. . . ." I give him what's supposed to be a meaningful stare. "Choose a movie! Or a TV show! Or even a concert. What do you want to watch?"

He studies me, eyes slightly widened.

"How—I don't get you, Natalie. I really don't."

I poke his shoulder, only vaguely aware this is the third time I've poked him within the last five minutes. "Aw, c'mon, William. Is it really that hard to believe I want my fake boyfriend to have an okay experience flying? Except for terrifying you a second ago, which is beside the point."

William shakes his head. I'm not sure whether he's saying no to this or no to whatever's on his mind. Then he sighs and looks at me with new energy.

"Okay. Let's watch movies. And then sleep. And then wake up back in Europe."

"Portugal!" I exclaim. "I love it. Their beaches. Their food, William! Their food is fabulous. Their colonization history, not so much."

That gets him to laugh.

A caught-off-guard laugh that makes him let go of his armrests for a moment.

It's hard to compare anything to the pride I feel when I steal one of these laughs from him. Maybe only performing can top it. It makes me feel like I can do anything.

"You choose the first film," he says.

I suck my bottom lip, viewing the screen, then glance back at him. "So I saw before that they had a cool action movie in the catalogue. . . ."

"If we're watching a mindless action film first, then our second film has to be an award-winning drama," he announces.

He isn't holding on to anything anymore. He seems more concerned with being forced to watch car chases for the next hour and a half.

I offer my hand. "Deal."

Early November in Faro, Portugal, isn't as cold as the rest of Europe, but it's still colder than I was expecting. There's no mob of photographers to receive us at the airport, so we make a stop at a nearby shop to buy coats.

"What do you think of this one?" I offer up a heavy brown coat in his general direction and he makes a face. "What? It's cute! You have to at least try it on."

William takes the coat and puts it over his shoulders without even bothering to put his arms in the sleeves. Then he walks closer to one of the wall-length mirrors, and poses. "Yep. I look like a grandfather, like I thought I would."

I take the coat back from him, frowning. "It's classy!"

He wrinkles his nose and puts it back on the hanger.

I appear by his side and drop another coat on his shoulders. This one is cream-colored, and goes down to his knees. It's the height of European fashion, and he looks so handsome in it. When I take a step back and say "Twirl!" he turns around with an unexplainable duck face, and I break down laughing. "Stop! It's a nice coat!"

He smiles, taking it off again. "I do believe it's nice on a number of people who aren't me."

"You're too difficult," I say, moving on to the more feminine coats. I have enough of essentially everything plaid, so I keep searching until I find a stunning solid pearl-colored coat that I like. I don't have to try it on. I hand it to the shop assistant and tell her I won't need a bag.

William doesn't seem to have even noticed me buying my coat.

He's still going through the racks, a frown of concentration on his face. He looks so vulnerable and open like this . . . focused under the bright shopping lights, like he's doing something utterly complicated.

"Um . . ." I pause, stopping next to a rack of black coats. I find the simplest one. It's thick and goes down probably until a little above his knees, with big black buttons and two front pockets. It's practical and beautiful. I examine the coat further as I start toward him. "William . . ."

He turns around and suddenly we're only inches away from each other.

I hold the coat closer to my body, eyebrows raised and a question on my lips.

His pale face turns pink and his Adam's apple bobs.

"I—should I try this one?" he asks, voice rough. He clears his throat, and when he takes the coat from me, our fingers brush.

My chest feels tight. Something warm settles in my stomach.

I nod, letting go of the coat and taking two steps back.

William takes a deep breath and inspects the coat at eye level. There's a small smile on his lips as he tries it on, properly this time. He's so handsome. The expression on his face is something else. As he moves closer to the mirror, he keeps looking back at me and grinning, like he doesn't believe he's found *the one*.

The one coat that his picky self is okay with, I mean.

"I love it"—he spreads his arms—"it's *nice!*"

I hang back, watching him in front of the mirror.

There's an instinct in me, a need to turn around and search for photographers or fans. Is he putting on a show for an audience? But there's only four or so people in the shop right now, and not even the shop assistant seems really that interested in us.

He's just happy. Not for anyone's sake but his own.

"Hi." He turns toward the shop assistant. "How much is this, please?"

Before she can answer, I'm shuffling to find my card in my purse.

"I'm paying! It's my treat! I'll pay for both!"

William tilts his head to the side. "You already picked a coat?"

I nod, and then start toward the cashier.

William elbows me lightly. "I'm paying for dinner, then."

I like the promise of dinner.

As we leave the airport shop, I spot a couple of fans snapping a picture or two, but it's not intrusive, and we don't comment on it. Soon we're headed to the hotel. In the car, I tell him Padma is already waiting for us in the lobby, and he gives me a curious look.

"So I'm meeting your friends in a few minutes?"

I frown back at him, then gesture at his face. "If I didn't know any better, I'd say that you're shy about it. Are you going to blush when you meet them?" I tease, and when he rolls his eyes and laughs, I bump my shoulder to his. "Are you? Are you?"

"You're impossible, Natalie."

But he says it with a smile that's just for me.

We're stuck in traffic for a little while, and the cabdriver comments that it's because of the festival. Too many tourists during the summer, he tells me. The beaches attract too many vacationers.

Does he think we don't qualify as tourists because I speak some Portuguese?

"What did he say?" William asks, a little quieter.

"Nothing much. Said that you smell and he'd like you out of his car."

With the earnest expression he's had all day, he pokes me. Right in the middle. Like I poked him on the airplane. Ticklish, I slap his hand away, and he says, "I'm so done with you today. You're too happy, and I've come to realize that's annoying."

And I realize he's right. I am happy. When we're quiet for the rest of the ride to the hotel, it feels good.

I risk resting my head on his shoulder like we did at the movies. He puts an arm around my shoulders and wordlessly runs his fingers through my hair, looking out at the old city as we drive by. I smile the whole time.

The hotel is wonderful, but the best thing about it is entering the lobby and spotting one of my best friends, wearing a neon-pink top, neon-green oversize jacket that looks like it's made of plastic, and black leather pants. She's absolutely gorgeous.

"Padma!"

She spreads her arms and hugs me so tight she might break my bones. She lifts me off my feet as William enters carrying our two bags. When we separate, I still have an arm around her. "You look so beautiful, oh my God. You look *incredible.*"

"I look like the headliner I am, Natalie. That's what I look like." Then she grabs my shoulders and in a goofy voice says, "I look like *money!*"

William laughs a little, too. "How long has it been since you guys last saw each other?"

We pull back and look at each other. "Two weeks?" I ask.

"Two weeks," she confirms. He chuckles, and she lets me go, pushing me aside not-so-gently. "Bring it in, Ainsley!" She spreads her arms again.

He blinks, apparently surprised.

"Don't tell me you're too British for hugs!" Padma teases.

That makes William smile, and as he goes closer, he announces, "I find that particularly stereotypical and offensive."

She takes him into her arms, and it's weird but in a good way. When they separate, she asks, smirking, "Do you want to talk to the Pakistani girl about what's stereotypical and offensive?"

A little embarrassed and a little amazed, he shakes his head. "Better not, I'm afraid."

"This is Padma, DJ Lotus, one of the coolest people you'll ever meet," I tell him.

William nods at that. "So I see."

"And this"—I turn to Padma, pointing at William—"is . . . William. William Ainsley, as you know. Great actor. My PR boyfriend for the moment. My friend."

"That's a weird introduction," Padma murmurs, snorting.

William turns to me. "Not one of the coolest people she'll ever meet?"

I make a face. "Eh."

Without warning, he puts his arm around my shoulders again. I swallow the little noise that comes up to my throat. My eyes widened, I mouth, *What?!* to Padma as I settle into the pseudo-hug.

I'm not complaining.

I can see something out of the corner of my eye. I bring my hand up as though running my fingers through my hair, but instead I take a look at the woman in her early twenties by the stairs with a phone pointed toward us.

It makes me suddenly uncomfortable. Has William noticed it? Is that why he's acting so nice to Padma? To me? I mean, he *is* nice. Generally. But has he seen her, too? Is he smiling for the sake of the camera?

Padma takes a deep breath.

"Listen, friends, go have dinner and get settled and all of that. The festival's starting soon. *But* I do have to warn you about one thing. And I'm sorry about it." Her face tells me she's not. "You called at the last possible minute, and

I'd already arranged for Brenda's sister to come with her husband and all . . ."

"Are we sleeping on your floor?" I eye her.

"Nothing like that, you silly girl." Padma shakes her head. "It's just that there was only one suite left. Soyou-havetoshare," she adds quickly, before either of us can react.

Suddenly I'm very self-conscious of how William's holding me.

His touch burns. Or perhaps it's my face burning.

I think William feels it, too, because he makes it his mission to pick up the bags. *Now.*

"I'll sleep on the floor," he announces, and makes a move toward the elevator. "Cool? So let's go? See you soon, Padma?"

Every single thing he says sounds like a question.

I nod at William, and then I swing toward Padma and mouth, *I will kill you.*

She gives me her Miss Pakistan wave.

On our way up, on the elevator, I call Mom. She answers on the first ring, and I chuckle. "Were you waiting for my call?"

"Like you used to wait for more *Cordel Encantado* episodes when you were little, yes. Anxiously," she clarifies, and I hear her laugh on the other side. "Are you at the hotel?"

"Yes . . ." I trail off. William gestures for me to keep talking, and grabs the bag from my hands as soon as the doors slide open. I bite back a smile watching him lead the way, and step out of the elevator, too. "Um, everything okay. Everything good."

"How's your boyfriend?" she asks.

My cheeks heat up, and I stare at him, wide-eyed, even though I don't think he heard it. He's scrambling for the key card, but I still turn around, making a shelf with my hand so he can't hear it, and whisper an offended "Mamis. Don't!"

She properly laughs at that. "All right, I was waiting for your call before starting this new project, but I have to go to the drawing board to try to hack what the client wants. Have fun at the festival!"

My heart warms as much as my face hearing her laugh. We say our goodbyes with William a few feet ahead, and he enters the room first.

He stands in the entryway and checks the room number against the key. "I can't believe this is a hotel room. No, it isn't, is it?" He turns to me. "It's a hotel *apartment*. It's too big. Like, I cannot comprehend how big this is." He lets go of the bags and spreads his arms.

I laugh, taking off my new coat. "It's not that big of a deal, but I'm glad you like it."

His eyes sweep over me, but then he looks away and drops on the couch like he belongs there. "I can sleep in the living room. You take the bedroom, obviously. I wouldn't make you sleep out here."

The couch is beautiful, with a carved wooden back and

plump cushions, but it's still a love seat. There's no way his lanky body will fit.

"Let's get ready to go, and we'll decide who sleeps where later, all right?"

William nods. "I——" Then he stops himself.

I narrow my eyes. "You . . . ?"

"You know what?" He raises his eyebrows. "It's nothing. It's whatever."

I shake my head; he doesn't get out of this that easy. I sit on the couch next to him. "Mom always says this thing. Começou termina. If you start saying something, you have to finish. It's impolite otherwise."

He chuckles. "It's just——thank you. For taking me here. It'll be good to focus on something else that isn't my family's financial issues or Cedrick talking about how great of an opportunity it'd be to sign this ridiculously long contract. I still don't know what to do about that."

I think back on Bobbi's offer for my next album.

"Yeah. Don't thank me yet. You haven't seen me out on the town." I raise an eyebrow at him and do a little shimmy. "Party animal over here."

He makes a pretend-serious face, sizing me up. "I don't quite believe you."

"Can I say something unrelated?" I ask, and then bulldoze on. "I do not hate your socks. I don't. But I hope you're not wearing them to the beach tonight. Socks and sand don't go together."

William properly laughs at that, then gives me a funny look.

"Maybe I have some interesting socks planned for the festival. Maybe they're neon. Maybe they light up." He studies my reaction, then rolls his eyes. "You're too easy! No, of course I'm not wearing socks to the beach. I actually didn't mind the outfit for the film premiere, either. It was the way Ashley talked to me. Like I needed to be molded into something I'm not."

I nod slowly.

Before I know it, I'm telling him, "That day at the People's Choice Awards, before everything, I presented this award. Best TV Drama. And this girl . . . she's one of the lead actors, right? And she linked her arm with mine, or I linked my arm with hers. The whole time we were hugging. I don't even know her name."

William doesn't say anything, but his eyes soften as if he gets it. And I think he does.

I should say something to fill in the serious silence, otherwise he may blurt out something silly like how we all don't need fame, etc. So I say, "But anyway, at the premiere . . . You looked good."

William cocks an eyebrow. "Oh. Is that a compliment?"

I roll my eyes, then look him up and down. "Grow up. I'm stating a fact. An obvious fact." That seems to shock him out of jokes, but I'm not done yet. "Just like it's obvious that I looked incredible. And you should have told me so."

"You're gorgeous, Natalie."

Scanning his face for any sign of sarcasm, my face warms when I see the truth in his deep green eyes.

I bite my cheek, even though Brenda has warned me against it. "That's not what I meant. I wasn't fishing for compliments."

William smiles. A pure, simple smile. "I know. I should have told you then, but I'm telling you now, you looked incredible that night. You *are* incredible."

For a second, my heart stutters in my chest. And our giant suite? Suddenly feels like extremely close quarters.

It's going to be an *interesting* weekend.

Chapter 18

This Is New for Me

illiam lets me take a shower first, and when I leave the bathroom, I'm already wearing my festival outfit: a white button-down shirt with a black lacy bralette underneath and skinny jeans. My hair is still mostly straight, but after the humidity of the shower, my curly baby hairs make an appearance.

I try not to spend too long in front of the bathroom mirror, working on winged eyeliner and a nude lipstick. I apply mascara and a bit of concealer and powder before all that, going for a more natural beach look.

My mascara is waterproof, though. These lashes are staying long, curled, and dark, no matter what.

But I'm feeling pretty as I step out of the enormous bathroom. I don't see William in the living room or the bedroom, and I'm starting to worry he might've ditched me when I find him on the balcony of the suite, moving plates and cutlery from a little table back to our room.

"What are you doing?" I raise my eyebrows.

William blinks a few times, like I've caught him doing something nasty. He stands up straight, puts down the cutlery on the balcony table, and stretches the back of his head. "I . . . was thinking maybe we could have dinner outside. But it's kind of cold, and that was a bad idea, so I'm moving it back inside."

My face burns, and I bite the insides of my cheeks.

"That's . . ." *Cute.* "Did you order room service for us?"

He nods, gathering up the cutlery again. I know I'm probably supposed to help him set the table, but I'm transfixed by the sight of him intently moving everything. "Yeah, of course. I did say dinner was on me. Plus I figured you wouldn't want to have dinner at a restaurant. Too many people, right?"

Too many people . . . and too many possibilities for our pictures to be snapped and posted online. Then again, it would be such great free publicity—us sharing a romantic dinner in a five-star hotel facing the ria in Faro before our friend's show.

His plan sounds so much better.

I smile, nodding slowly. "Do you need help, or—?"

"I got it, don't worry," he replies, and closes the balcony behind him, finally turning to me. He looks me up and down, then seems to think that's inappropriate and shakes his head. I bite back another smile, and he says, "I wasn't sure what you'd like, but I asked for the specialty of the house, if that's okay?"

I move to the table, but he cuts me off. I'm about to ask why he's being such a weirdo when he pulls out the chair for me. It feels like my heart is going to catapult out of my chest. I smile at him, mouthing a thank-you and sitting down. He goes to the other side of the table.

Between us are two closed dishes on black iron pans, two sets of plates with cutlery, and red wine glasses filled with water. I cock an eyebrow and take my glass. William quickly adds, "They asked me if I wanted some vinho do Porto, but I Googled it and it's like twenty percent alcohol! So I passed on that."

I laugh at his surprise. I've never had that kind of wine, but Mom loves it. I sort of want to tell him that, sort of want to tell him that he's wonderful. I've never really been in a situation like this before. Not alone in a hotel room with a flustered boy who keeps looking around like he's forgetting something.

The only thing that's missing is the dimmed lights, but I'll take it.

I'll take tonight exactly as it is.

Maybe *that's* something I could write about.

"Water's perfect," I say. "Tim tim," I say, cheersing in Portuguese, and he clinks his glass against mine.

We don't break eye contact as we drink our water. I

forget about Bobbi's proposition and even about Padma's upcoming show. I forget about the problems I've had writing lyrics in the past months, and I forget about my public persona.

I put the glass back on the table, and tilt my head to the side, eyeing the closed dishes. "And what do we have here?"

"I don't know, the lad assured me it was the best, but—" he starts, and I interrupt him by pulling off the lids.

The larger pan contains some delicious cataplana, and the smaller pan has white rice. It's cataplana de marisco, essentially a stew with seafood, with lots of tomatoes, tempero verde, and onions.

"Mmmm," I say, more to myself than him, but he laughs approvingly. "I've only had cataplana with pork before, so this is going to be new for me."

He smiles. "Yeah. This is new for me, too."

We exchange a long look, and my heart skips a beat.

It doesn't feel like we're talking about the Portuguese dish anymore.

But I smile politely and serve myself. I also serve him. I'm craving some migas to go with the dish, but I don't tell him that because I don't want him to think that this isn't the most perfect thing anyone's ever done. Which it probably is.

I'm so happy it feels like I could burst.

We make small talk. I ask him if he's ever been to Portugal before, and he says Lisbon's been on his list for forever, but Faro hadn't been on his radar. I ask about his favorite things in London, and as he gets excited and starts talking about streets and corners and indie pubs, I start paying attention to his mannerisms instead of his words. The way he gestures widely when he's excited. How his smile as he's talking is slightly lopsided.

My perfect fake boyfriend.

My . . .

We're on our second serving when both our phones beep loudly, mine from the purse near the door, his from the love seat. We pause, looking in their general direction.

"That was weird," I murmur.

"At the same time, yeah," he murmurs back.

I know nothing good can come of this. And I want to live in this moment for a little while longer. But William excuses himself and brings our phones to the table.

When he hands me my phone, our hands touch, but barely. His is a little cold.

He raises his eyebrows and looks at his phone first.

I watch the color drain out of his face, his mouth agape.

"What is it?" I ask, but my voice is just above a whisper. All I have to do is check.

I unlock my phone and see an email from Ashley to both of us. In her message, she apologizes for not having seen this coming, and says they will do everything in their power to disprove it, but doesn't say what *it* is. Below her little apologetic text is a link.

Holding my breath, I click it.

It's an article from the *Sun*, which reads: WILLIAM AINSLEY'S FAMILY BANKRUPT: THE INDIE ACTOR TRIES TO RIDE NATALIE'S FAME AND FORTUNE.

I put my phone down.

"William."

He's still reading. His Adam's apple bobs, and he breathes out slowly through his mouth. "This isn't happening," he says. I reach out for him across the table. When his eyes meet mine, he chuckles mirthlessly. "Yeah, this is new for me, definitely."

"Ashley will fix it," I reassure him, but his eyes are still panicked. He puts down his phone, parting his lips. My own heart is racing, so I can only imagine what he must be feeling. "This is nothing, okay? Nobody really buys that kind of thing. People speculate about stuff like this *all the time*. And they base these opinions on things like follower count or net worth, and—"

"It doesn't feel like nothing." William looks away from me, and when I try to hold his shaking hands, he pulls them away. I frown, but sit back on my chair. "This isn't speculation. They have documents about the loans Dad took before he passed. All the debt we accumulated after he died as well." He pauses, looks at me, face pale, voice a bit louder. "How did they even find these? Who leaks stuff like that?"

"I don't know, and I'm so sorry, but I promise it's going to be okay."

I feel so weird sitting on the other side of the table, like we're on a phone call from different sides of the world. I'm not sure he's even listening to me. He's looking through me, like he's mentally taking stock of a thousand things. I want to fix this. I want it to stop.

I knew we shouldn't have checked our phones.

"I need to call Mum," he says, getting up suddenly. I get up, too.

"Do you want me to . . ." I search my brain, trying to be useful. *Think, Natalia, think.* "Do you want me to let you be alone for a bit?"

William nods, looking at the phone in his hands. "Yeah, maybe you can go ahead and meet your friends for the festival? I promise I'm joining you soon. I want to talk to Mum and my sister Amanda, and then I'll take a quick shower and meet you there. Thanks."

All I want to do is help, but I can't—not when I'm part of the problem.

I nod. "Sure," I say quietly. I put on my shoes and coat, and leave him.

I notice he waits until I'm out the door to make the call.

Chapter 19

A Serious Evil-Mermaid Move

Past the Ria Formosa and the city, the stage faces the ocean. In the VIP area, my friends and I are eating pastel de nata and watching the ocean turn to neon colors as the lights of the festival spread way beyond the crowds. It's a nice kind of calm, sitting side by side with our coats forgotten in the small six-person VIP suite that Padma got for us. To the other side, we can see the stage; right now DJ X-Perenss is mixing the summer's biggest pop hits, creating a parallel universe, where only tonight exists.

But the mood is off. Over the music, over the excitement, over the smell of the dried ice and pot, I exchange a look with William, and even though he's mid-shrimp bite, he smiles back at me, but it feels hollow. He just got here, maybe a full half hour after me, looking a little lost and out of place. When I asked him how the call went, he said, *Well, don't worry.*

I am absolutely worried.

"You've been weirdly quiet," Padma announces.

I turn around. She's sitting on one of the black satin couches that frame our space. There are white curtains separating us from the rest of the VIP area as well, and a small island of champagne, vodka, and Red Bulls in the center.

Brenda's mixing an energy drink with champagne. I frown at that, until I realize she's using the champagne glass, not pouring in the champagne. Which would probably taste awful and be totally out of character for Brenda.

Dropping next to her on the couch, I say, "Just thinking about things. I don't know. Relationships are complicated, even if they're . . . fake."

Padma looks at William, his elbows resting on the balcony of the suite, looking past the frenetic crowd to the ocean. Brenda elbows him in the middle, and he turns to her with wide eyes. She offers him a champagne glass's worth of energy drink. "William, my man! Tell me what you think of the festival so far."

Their voices fade until they become background noise, along with the music. Padma chuckles and shakes her head.

"I wish I could have what you and Brenda have. You two are perfect for each other."

I'm thinking out loud—I know these aren't fair expectations, and to be honest, nothing makes me happier than the happiness of those I love. But Padma seems to think it's funny. She throws a leg over the other side of the couch, taking twice as much space as me, and takes a sip of her energy drink.

"Nobody is perfect for anybody. You have to do the work."

But it's simpler in her case. It has to be. Because there are no contracts and it's their choice to be with each other and the tabloids never seem to care much about Brenda. That lack of attention is probably liberating.

Being a very famous pop star and a very famous DJ comes with very different types of attention.

I don't say any of that. I look at her, lips parted, and before I can organize my thoughts, she tells me, "Brenda's freaking out about college because she's afraid we might break up. If she gets into Berkeley, she's going to have to study harder than she has all her life, and I'm going on an international tour for six months while she'll be stressed out in a college campus." Padma's eyes venture toward Brenda and William, deep in conversation, and she adds, "We're not going to break up. We love each other. But it'll be hard."

I'm quiet for a second, regretting my words. When did everything get so complicated?

"I'll be there for both of you. I promise," I say.

Padma nods, smiling. "We know that. What means the

most is just being here. I don't like to talk about everything the way Brenda does. . . . I need you to be by my side. By our side. And you are."

Without warning, I pull her into a hug.

It's sudden and makes her nearly lose balance, but after the initial surprise, she hugs me back, hard. I try to transmit all my love for her into that hug. I think she gets it.

When we pull away, she touches my shoulder so I don't go too far. "It'll be okay with William, too. Let yourself forget all the problems tonight. Be one with the night."

If anybody else was saying that, it would sound cliché and weird, but this is Padma, with her serious eyes and her million rings, her nearly fully pierced ear and her fixation with the dark hours and loud music. When her face breaks into a smile, I smile, too.

We're quiet for a second, sitting side by side, watching Brenda and William talk. She looks serious, but the way he throws his head back in laughter means she's probably telling a very elaborate joke.

His laughter is so contagious that I can't help smiling.

"Beautiful, right?" Padma asks, her voice just above a murmur.

I blink a few times. Brenda. She's talking about Brenda.

She *is* beautiful—and she's especially cute in this loose, shimmery golden dress that flows down until it hits the middle of her thighs. But my eyes are on him. William wears a black button-down shirt with the sleeves rolled up, and dark blue jeans with holes in them. He's barefoot, his shoes forgotten next to our coats, along with my platform high heels and Brenda's ballerina shoes.

He catches me staring and winks at me. Like he's saying, *Everything's going to be all right.* And I feel myself letting out a breath.

I would very much like to kiss that birthmark on his cheek.

And then he's back in conversation with Brenda, giving her his full attention.

"So beautiful," I agree.

There's something wonderful about burying your toes in the sand, your pants rolled up enough that you can feel the breeze tickle your ankles as you approach the seashore. I know there's a special feeling there—something that surpasses the fireworks as the festival hits its second hour and someone with a grave voice announces that it's time for DJ Lotus to take this festival to the next level.

William and I left Brenda at the VIP section as Padma rushed us out to get prepared for her show, but we also accidentally left our shoes and coats there. We passed through the crowd without anyone spotting us—if people care about who we are, they're too busy dancing to stop us—and headed straight for the most secluded area, close to the shoreline, where the waves are breaking.

"Not a fantastic idea to leave our coats there," I say, wrapping my arms around myself. My white T-shirt is *not* enough to keep me warm.

William jogs ahead of me and lifts his shoulder. "I guess the only thing to do is dance. Either dance, or freeze."

My eyes widen, and I shake my head. "I'm like Adele, darling. I don't do dancing!"

"Oh, darling," he repeats, apparently very proud that I've used his weapon against himself. "Watch and learn." Then he stops in front of me and starts dancing.

Or, well, some version of dancing.

He throws his arms around to the electronic music, not making much sense, but it does make me smile. Somewhere between the VIP area and here, William has started to seem more like himself. I appreciate the effort, or maybe this is normal for him. Being present, living in the moment. Either way I want to wrap my arms around his neck and tell him that everything will be okay.

But I'm game for staying in the present and being here with him.

By the time the first song ends, he's jumping nonstop. Padma smoothly transitions to the remix of my song.

His jaw drops, and he yells, "'Together Forever'! It's your song!"

I nod, endeared by his reaction.

"You can't deny me this dance," he says, offering me his hand.

The first verse starts, and Padma's beats are a crescendo that culminate with the pre-chorus. I decide to let go. First I close my eyes, and then I let my hand find his.

In spite of the cold, his hand is so warm.

With my eyes closed, I let the beats move through me. I find the rhythm or the rhythm finds me, and either way we become one: the song and I. When I open my eyes, William is looking at me in a way he never has before. There's a hint of a grin there, but his eyes are the darkest green they've ever been, and when he touches the small of my back to bring me closer, I swear that we're the only ones in the whole entire world.

His lips brush my ear as we're moving when he says, "I guess you *do* dance, darling."

I lean back, closer to him. "I guess I do. *Darling.*"

He laughs at the way I mimic his accent, but we keep dancing like our bodies wouldn't know what to do if they were apart.

When the music ends, Padma screams into the microphone, "Faro, Portugal, how's it going?! I am DJ Lotus, and we're here to have a good time!"

We break apart slowly.

My shirt is clinging to my chest with sweat, but there's something magical happening that I can't quite put my finger on. Behind the stage, the fireworks explode, coloring the sky way beyond the neon lights. The crowd cheers, and I cheer, too, just as loudly, just as intensely.

Looking up at the sky, I see that a storm is coming.

Still, I spread my arms, bathing in the energy of the night.

The songs come one after the other, Padma keeping the crowd hyped through every minute, and I register for the thousandth time why she's so good at what she does. It's more than her set. It's her energy, making the whole beach pulsate as one while we all dance to her music. I dance with William and around him, and we laugh and when we stop, our smiles linger. It feels like dinner is a thousand miles away, and nothing can bring us down tonight.

It's maybe an hour later when William runs by me and straight into the water. "No!" I yell, but I'm laughing, too. "You're going to get soaked!" He kicks up the water in the shallows so that it cascades down around him.

"Look around, Natalie," he yells back at me. The approaching storm colors the sky in the darkest hues of blue, the clouds heavy and a dark gray. "We're all going to get soaked in seconds."

The music starts pulsating through me, and I want to give in and dance, but he's right. I feel the first few raindrops falling on my face, and instead of running for cover, like a few from the crowd do, I smile even bigger.

"It's so cold!"

I only hear William's laughter in response. I turn to him, and he's staring up at the moon; his pale skin flushed, his dark curls sticking to his forehead. He catches me staring, and his face turns serious.

He comes closer, and I feel my heart thud inside my chest.

William's only a foot away from me when he pauses . . . and kicks the water so high that I'm hit with a shower of salty water. "You jerk!" I accuse, scream-laughing, chasing after him as he runs away. "You think you're so funny? You think you're hilarious?"

I kick the water so it soaks him, too.

We end up farther out into the sea, so the waves lap at our shins. There's something thrilling about being on the water in a storm, the rain merciless. I stop in front of him, ready to give him the final kick of water that will wipe that smirk off his face.

His eyes widen. I only have time to see the swear forming on his lips before a wave knocks into him and he falls backward.

I've seen enough novelas to know the guy *always* catches the girl when she's falling.

I'm a feminist. I can do this. I clumsily reach out and grab his arms as he starts falling, but I only manage to pull his weight in my direction instead.

"Oh no." I don't know who says it—both of us?—but I'm still clinging to him for dear life when *I* fall back in the water.

My soaked clothes drag me down. I thrash and try to scream, water getting in my mouth as I feel myself sink.

"Help!"

At first I think William's helping me, but then I realize he can't stop laughing. "What are you doing? It's shallow! Just sit."

Sitting up, I realize the water only goes to my belly.

But it's still soaked through my clothes.

It's funny how I don't feel too self-conscious about the lacy black bralette under my shirt. It's—I don't know. I like that he looks down at the clothes hugging my figure and then up at my face again, like he isn't sure how to proceed. It makes me sit a little taller.

I want him to see me.

"Useless boy," I mutter playfully. I grab his shoulder so I can push him away.

He nearly falls to the side again. Still laughing, he shakes his head, then runs his hands over his hair to push it away from his eyes. "What *was* that, anyway?"

"I was saving you," I say, doing the same to my hair. I can feel the curls in my hands. "Obviously." I roll my eyes at him, and for good measure, stick out my tongue.

He sticks out his tongue as well.

"How mature, William!" I accuse.

He doesn't reply. He's just looking at me.

I want him to keep looking at me that way.

He tilts his head up at the sky and closes his eyes.

The rain is hitting our faces, and I'm cold, but the ocean makes us warmer.

It's different from anything else I've experienced.

It's liberating.

He finally stands up and offers me a hand. "C'mon, you're going to catch a cold."

I cross my arms over my chest. "You don't get to tell me what to do!"

I bite back a smile and watch him groan in frustration.

"Fine," he says, and without warning, his hands go to my middle.

I react with a scandalized scream as he lifts me out of the water and throws me over his shoulder.

A few people turn to see what's going on, but when they see a soaked couple emerging from the water and giggling, I suppose they don't care much about it.

"Put me down!" I yell, hitting his back. But I don't mind this one bit—his warm hand around my waist, his throaty laugh. When he does put me down gently on the beach, I adjust my clothes, shaking my head, and tell him, "Deplorable, William. You're like a caveman."

"Let's go back to the hotel, cavewoman." He continues walking, and I jog up to meet him. "Before, you know, you die and the tabloids say I drowned you or something."

I bump my shoulder against him. "Dark."

He turns to me, beaming like only he can do. "Yeah, especially since you were the one pulling me into the water, actually. That was a serious evil-mermaid move."

I grin.

As Padma says her goodbye to Faro and thanks them for a fantastic night, we make our way back to the hotel side by side, the rain dancing on our skin and making us feel completely alive.

Chapter 20

Seen Just Now

The shower feels like the most magnificent thing that has ever happened to me. I lower my head and let the water wash the salt out of my hair until I can almost see my worries going down the drain.

It's a bright marble bathroom, so bright that it hurts my eyes a little—white tiles, white ceiling, white floor. But if I close my eyes, I can imagine there's just me and the water.

I wrap my arms around myself.

William knocks. "Natalie, I'm dying out here! Just finish your shower already!"

I open the glass shower door to yell back, "You're the one who insisted I go first!"

I can picture him running his hands through his curls.

"I was being a gentleman! Now I'm too frozen to be a gentleman! I'm going to be a full-on penguin when you finally leave the bathroom."

I smile, turning off the shower.

Stepping out, I grab a huge fluffy white towel to wrap around my head and wrap another around my body.

"You're such a baby," I tell William as I open the door.

He's rendered speechless, apparently. Taking two steps back, he gapes at me. "Ah . . . ?"

I adjust the towel around my body so it's firm. I look down. Nothing scandalous about the towel, everything covered, nothing out of place. "What?"

William blinks at me.

I snap my fingers in front of him. "Weren't you dying from cold?"

Clearing his throat, he turns to get a change of clothes, passes me to go to the bathroom, and slams the door shut dramatically on his way in.

I cock an eyebrow. The smell of salt water still lingers.

I sit on the bed, taking off the towel from around my head. My curls are in full power. I forgot my straightener. But it's also kind of late and I don't care much. I start combing through my hair, trying to push away thoughts that seem particularly inconvenient now.

But the look on his face when he saw me . . .

And then I realize what should have occurred to me earlier. I run to my bag, get my phone, and unlock it. I click to my photo gallery, but new pictures don't magically appear. I hadn't been thinking about photo ops after Ashley sent that article, and then . . .

We had so much fun. We were so magical and happy. Tonight would've made amazing pictures. So many likes, maybe a new trending hashtag.

I hold my phone.

Is it bad that I don't regret it? Not taking pictures? Even if I know I should've?

Ashley is going to be so disappointed.

And I can't pretend to care.

Mom has texted me to ask about the show, so I quickly text her back to tell her how great it was. After choosing comfy pajamas, I hop on the bed again, and send Padma a voice message, saying that she killed it tonight.

I eye the bathroom door suspiciously, but I can still hear the shower.

If I'd known we'd be sharing a room, maybe I would've packed something a little cuter than flannel pajamas—plaid red-and-black bottoms and a gray top with a pocket in the front. But that's what I got, so to distract myself, I open Twitter.

I don't have to go very far to see a video from half an hour ago, when William threw me over his shoulder. I click the video so that I can see it again and again and again. He's smiling so smugly and I'm laughing so much. And we are thoroughly wet from the impromptu swim in the ocean.

I minimize the video. The caption reads: SEEN JUST NOW. NATALIE AND WILLIAM AINSLEY.

I don't even have to tell my finger to click the replies— it's automatic.

There are a lot of GIF reactions. Most of them show cartoons swooning. Some of them show actual people swooning. Someone has a screenshot of William's biceps. Actually, there are a lot of comments about his biceps.

I imagine the feel of his muscles under my fingertips....

Clearing my throat, I keep scrolling down.

NATAFAN #STOPTRANSPHOBIA

@erin_natafan
SHE IS SO HAPPY OMG LOOK AT OUR QUEEN!!!
she was never like that with trent lmao

I grip my phone. I feel something familiar in my chest, a nervous flutter I've felt for a while. Because none of them know that it isn't real.

And that I *want* it to be real.

Though I try swallowing the knot in my throat, it's difficult.

Eventually, William opens the door and comes out dressed in a *Rolling Stones* black T-shirt and a pair of gray sweatpants. No socks, surprisingly. Hair slicked back and still wet and so charming that the only reason I don't smile when I see him is that he's frowning.

"Can you believe how hot that shower gets? I got *burned*!"

I snort. "You're very white. I imagine you get burned all the time. Every time you step into the sun."

He closes the door behind him, shaking his head. "Now, that's reverse racism." I sit up, ready to argue, and he starts laughing at me. "JK, obviously! There's no such thing as reverse racism. Don't throw anything at me."

I lock the phone's screen and put it away. "I would never. I'm a lady."

"Sure."

I get up from the bed and gesture toward the balcony. He follows me wordlessly. The knot keeps rising and making me want to say things that don't make sense, so I push it back down and focus on something else. "Those aren't proper pajamas. Do the British not believe in wearing pajamas?"

I sit in front of the balcony without daring to slide the glass doors open. It's still cold out there and inside we're favored by the gods of the heating system.

William sits by my side. "Quite the contrary. These *are* my pajamas."

"Of course they are." I give him a look.

"Anyway, it's a nice view. Faro Beach." He gestures at the view, and I nod, about to say something about Padma's set, when he says, "It's also nice to be here. With you, I mean."

My eyes stay on him.

"You mean, instead of some random terrible girl that you'd hate to be fake-dating?"

He shrugs. "Something like that," he says. "I was so reluctant to do this. . . . I didn't want to come to the States. I didn't want to sign that contract. Even with the money involved, I was so . . . I didn't want to open myself up to heinous, privacy-destroying articles like the one that ran in the *Sun*."

My blood turns cold. "William, I'm so deeply s—"

"I know. It's not your fault," he says, with a gentle smile. Then he looks at me. "What I wanted to say is that I guess I was very afraid."

That shuts me up. I suddenly understand why he wasn't looking at me before. I'm very interested in the pattern of my pajama pants now and how it feels under my hand.

"Afraid of being away from my family, afraid of not being able to be good enough to fit in. Afraid of spending so much time with someone I didn't know and worried whether I'd end up becoming friends with her or not." He shrugs. "But Cedrick kept telling me it was the right move. He also thought it was a good idea because . . . you're a girl."

My heart stops.

I swallow the damn knot and hold my breath.

"You're gay," I state matter-of-factly, feeling the floor underneath me shatter.

Feeling a lot of things shatter.

William turns to me with raised eyebrows. "I'm—? What? I'm not, actually."

I narrow my eyes, breathing in. "I'm . . . confused."

He cocks an eyebrow, leaning closer to me. "The B in the LGBTQIA acronym doesn't stand for baseball enthusiasts."

I take advantage of him being close to bump his shoulder. "William."

"I'm bisexual," he clarifies, still giving me a little knowing smile.

I roll my eyes. "Yeah. I got that."

My pajamas are suddenly very interesting. He's still looking at me.

"You have questions."

I sigh, risking a glance his way. "I do."

"Ask away." He makes a dorky welcome gesture.

He *is* dorky.

I clear my throat, then straighten my legs and pull them close to sit cross-legged. "I . . . I won't do that to you. I'll Google it first."

"You're going to Google the word *bisexual*?" He makes a strange noise. "Oh, I can tell you what it means."

It's just . . . I turn to him, my cheeks flushed, my heart beating fast.

"You really go hard with the dorkiness sometimes, don't you?" I glare, and he bows. "No. My best friend is bi, but I know it's not the same . . . since you're a guy. Different struggles and all. I mean—I'll do some research. I don't want you to have to school me on anything I can find online. I don't want to sound ignorant—which I sort of am, to be fair. But . . . Yeah. It's not fair to you. I don't want to be a bigot."

He looks at me as if that's new. He doesn't look like he's about to crack a joke anymore. He frowns slightly, and says, "I . . . appreciate you not wanting to be a bigot, I suppose."

"No problem." My turn to bow. "I guess I *am* the hero of this story."

William's smirk comes back. "An exceptional hero, of course."

"Are you out?" I blurt. Then I hasten to explain, "I hadn't heard anything about this."

"Have you been Googling me?" He raises an eyebrow. I stutter and he saves me with a smile. "Sort of. To my family and friends, yes. Cedrick knows, too, like I said. I'm not *not* out. But I guess I haven't given any interviews about it or anything."

We're close enough that I let my head fall onto his shoulder, and he lets me stay there. Quietly, I tell him, "Aren't you scared of the tabloids doing something about that?"

"Yes, I am." He leans closer so his head touches mine. "I don't want them to take away my choice to discuss my sexuality on my own terms. But I guess unless my ex-boyfriend decides to speak to the press, it's unlikely they'll find out."

I raise my head to look at him. We're closer than I'd anticipated, and I feel my face warm up. I clear my throat, but still sound a little strangled when I say, "Oh, so the . . . the ex you said that you deleted all the pictures from Instagram and stuff . . . that was . . . not a girl."

He shakes his head no, watching me. I can't tell if he's amused by me not having considered this, or by my current blushing situation, which isn't even about what he said. It's about how I can see every nuance in the color of his eyes.

I rest my head on his shoulder again, but it isn't as comfortable this time. I need him to stop looking at me like that. Above a whisper, I tell him, "Thanks for not being a bigot to me, either."

Lowering his head a little so he can speak in the same tone, he asks, "Are you coming out, too?"

I raise my head. "I—what? No, keep up, William!" I snap my fingers in front of his face again, and he laughs. I rest my head on his shoulder again. "I'm a Latina girl. I've heard all sorts of things. But you're cool."

He's quiet for a moment, before saying, "Do you want to share some horror stories?"

I close my eyes. There are so many to choose from.

"Well, there was this time a guy from my label promptly told me his wife loved Buenos Aires when he heard I was from Brazil."

"Isn't Buenos Aires in Arg—" he starts.

"Argentina, yes."

"Huh." William clicks his tongue. "Incredible sense of geography."

"This other time, but this was early on, right when we'd moved to the States, Mom took me to an office barbecue and this woman dead-ass asked Mom if she could cook chimichangas. When Mom gave her a blank stare, she specified: *Because you're, like, Brazilian, right?*"

It'd been a joke between Mom and me for a long time, though I'd known the comment had hurt anyway. It felt like a Brazilian thing, to deal with pain and stress through jokes. If you're not laughing, then you can't control how others will react.

William turns to me, the balcony forgotten. "Were they really a Valley Girl or is this just your default American accent?"

I consider this. "Default, I guess."

"Fair enough," he replies, still serious.

Groaning, I lean forward and hug my legs. "Why do some people think that all Latinx are Mexicans? Just one big homogenous group?"

"Racism? Xenophobia? Imperialism?"

I chuckle. "That was a rhetorical question."

"I know," he replies, a small smile on his lips, too.

"I'm glad Ashley connected Bobbi and Cedrick."

The words slip out of my lips. But I don't mind—it's something I have to say. I don't mind my damp hair curling, I don't mind my face free of makeup. This is me—the rawest, realest version of me.

He gives me a long look. "Me too."

"You know." I clear my throat, sitting up next to him. "As opposed to ending up with a complete asshole or something."

William brings his hands to his chest in fake shock. "You're calling me a *not* complete asshole? I am beyond flattered."

I shrug. "Don't get too used to it."

"Most certainly won't." He stands, and offers his hand to help me up. This time I take it.

His hand is warm and feels good in mine.

"You know how you called me Natalia before?" I ask.

He nods, standing too close.

I can feel the heat emanating off him. I want to lean closer.

"It *is* my name. When I came to the States, people found it so hard to pronounce properly. There's a nickname for my name, and it isn't Nat. It's Nati. But every kid in school pronounced it wrong."

"*Nah-tchy?*" he repeats.

The effort he seems to put in getting the pronunciation right makes me feel good. I nod slowly, lowering my head for a second. It's like staring at the floor makes me more self-aware of how close we are.

"Yeah. That's how you say it. I thought it'd be easier. Assimilating to the new culture, letting mine die a little every day. I think that's why I'm afraid of going back. Because I'm a little ashamed. I know in my heart that I tried to forget them."

He puts one hand on my arm.

A small encouragement to keep talking.

"I think I look beautiful," I say. He laughs, a little confused, so I explain. "I mean, with my hair like this. Natural. I'm all for people doing whatever to their hair so they feel good about themselves, but—but I don't want to straighten it anymore. I want people to see my hair the way it is."

One of William's hands goes to my face, hovering a few inches away from my cheek. Instead he touches a random curl, lightly as if to not undo what nature has done. "You *are* beautiful," he says simply.

I tilt my chin up, looking him in the eye.

"I'm done pretending to be someone I think they'll like better, William."

He smiles, his eyes focused on mine, like I'm the only thing in the world. It's enough.

Gathering my courage, I tell him, "You can call me Nati."

"Nice to meet you, Nati," he says just above a murmur.

My fingertips tingle. I want to touch him so bad. Hold his face, bring it close to mine, and . . .

My phone beeps. I shut my eyes and curse internally. It beeps again.

William clears his throat, puts some space between us, and says, "You should—you should probably get that."

I take a deep breath and go into the room, following my phone's increasing beeping.

It's the group chat with the girls.

PADMA:
AHHHHH
THAT WAS SO GOOD

BRENDA:
MY BABY KILLED IT!!!! IT WAS SO GOOD
SO
SO
SO
SO GOOD BABY

PADMA:
WHY ARE YOU TEXTING YOU'RE TWO
FEET AWAY FROM ME LOL

BRENDA:
sshhhhhhhhhhh
WHERE'S NATALIE AND WILLIAM

NATALIE:
safe and sound.
you were AMAZING, padma. :') <3

"Hey. Evil mermaid?" William appears by the door. "Can I steal a pillow?"

Putting my phone on silent mode, I toss it on my bag, hopefully buried under clothes where I will never hear it beep again. Now all my focus is on the handsome British guy in my room.

"What do you mean?"

William considers this. "To . . . sleep."

"I know 'to sleep.' I didn't think it was because you wanted to ride a horse. But where are you taking the pillow?"

Again, he looks clueless. "The couch . . . ? Didn't think you'd make me sleep in the lobby, but if that's what your heart desires, darling."

I cross my arms, raising my eyebrows. "Is it because I'm an evil mermaid? You're afraid I'll smother you with my pillow if you sleep next to me?"

His eyes widen slightly. "I hadn't considered that, so thanks for one more terrifying thing to think about before bed."

I shake my head, making a face. "I'm serious, though. You don't have to sleep on the couch. It's too small for you."

"I can handle it." He shrugs.

"No, stop." I start making a knot of my hair so it won't get on my face while I'm sleeping. "Stop being a baby and come to bed—" I pause, shutting my eyes. "I mean."

He's kind enough to ignore my wording. "You have

got to stop calling me a baby. I'll feel self-conscious of my manhood." He gestures to his chest.

"What's—" I mimic his gesture.

"My manly muscles, of course," William says with such a straight face that I can't help laughing.

Dork. Dork. Dork.

What am I doing?

I sigh. "Do you want the left or right side?"

Properly entering the room, he sighs. "I prefer left, thank you."

"No problem," I tell him.

What am I doing?

The mattress shifts underneath me as he climbs into bed. I'm still sitting up and staring ahead, and he clears his throat. "I should—I should probably turn off the light, though, right? Unless you don't want to go to sleep straight-away, which is okay—"

"Lights off, yes," I cut him off. Then, realizing I probably sound rude, I force a yawn. "I'm so . . . tired . . ."

Good thing he's the actor of the two of us.

Murmuring something unintelligible, William gets up again to turn off the light. As he passes in front of me, I lie down, staring at the ceiling and holding my breath. I only let it go when the whole room goes dark, the moonlight illuminating his silhouette softly as he comes back to bed. Next to me.

He's far away enough that I only feel the shift of the

mattress again, but I'm hyperaware of his presence next to me. We lie awkwardly beside each other in the dark, and maybe this was my worst idea yet. There's no way I'm going to be able to fall asleep.

"Um, good night, Nati," he says.

His voice is low and quiet, and it makes me want to turn to him. But instead I roll to my other side, away from him, my shoulders rigid. "Good night, William."

Then I prepare myself for a whole lot of counting sheep.

Chapter 21

Good Morning

I notice the weight around my shoulders first.

As I wake, I move my fingers slightly and realize I have a hand over William's stomach, which comes with the inevitable realization that my head is also on his chest.

My heart drums as I start to take in the details, my eyes still closed. His arm around my shoulders, keeping me close. My face half buried on his chest. The warmth that comes from him and not from the kicked-away blanket.

There's no going back now.

Not to sleep. And probably not to pretending we're just friends.

I open my eyes.

My fingers hover over his taut stomach, so as to not wake him, but I feel like I can't breathe until I see his face.

So I raise my head from his chest enough that I can look at him.

He seems peaceful, eyes closed and lips slightly parted, head tilted to the side. His hair is a mess. I want to run my fingers through his curls.

I want to hold his face.

I look away, trying to untangle from him so I can excuse myself to the bathroom, where I can have my existential crisis without waking him.

But his hold on my shoulders tightens a bit, and he frowns, pulling me in and nuzzling my neck. A shiver runs down my spine in response.

I'm caught mid-act, staring right at him, when he opens his eyes.

"Oh," he says. "Good morning?"

I cock an eyebrow, still not moving. "Good morning."

Neither of us moves.

He's wide-eyed. Terrified.

I swallow my feelings, and turn to leave.

"Wait," he asks quietly. "Nati."

I turn back to him, and the warmth bubbles back up, making it harder to breathe. I bite the insides of my cheeks as he gives me that long look I can't decode.

We're so close. . . .

"I wasn't going to run. I was just . . ."

"Going to run," he says. "Do you want to?"

I'm scared by how fast I shake my head no.

Hesitantly at first, he runs his fingers over my shoulder. I shiver, and glance at his hand as it slides down my arm, leaving a trail of heat behind it.

I meet his gaze. There's a question in them that he seems to be struggling to form with words.

But I know what it is.

Can we?

Should we?

I've been asking myself the same thing.

God. I care about him so much. I want him so bad.

I settle back into his arms. I can hear my heart beating fast, and I wonder if he can hear it, too. It's a time bomb, and I'm dying to see what happens when it goes off.

His other hand goes up to my hair and touches it lightly.

"I'm not running, either." And a little faintly, like he may regret it later, he says, "You're beautiful in every way. I'm done pretending I don't see it." I'm ready now, for whatever it is that comes next, but he's got one last thing to say. His face a little flustered, my own body in flames. "I fancy you, Nati."

I lean in closer to him, and when our noses touch, he takes a deep breath. I look him in the eye, my brown into his green, and I swear the world goes quiet.

He closes his eyes first. I close mine next.

And I touch my lips to his.

Lightly at first, our lips barely moving, hesitant, until he pulls me close and I press against him, my soft curves against his hard chest.

I deepen the kiss.

As our tongues slide together, my body finds a mind of its own, and the only thing it's thinking of is *William-WilliamWilliam*. I hold his face, run my fingers through his hair, kiss the curve of his mouth and the birthmark under his eye. He's smiling when he rolls me beneath him. Now he's on top of me, kissing my neck, trailing kisses up to my mouth.

When our lips meet again, it feels like we were meant to be here.

Like this.

I can hear the world trying to burst our bubble, but I won't let it. William pulls back, but I hum, not wanting our kiss to end. He holds me close, protectively now, as he turns to look at the entrance of the bedroom. Then he turns back to me with a cocked eyebrow.

Oh. So the world was literally trying to disrupt us. I didn't imagine the noise.

"I reckon . . . someone's knocking at the door?" he says.

I groan, and hop up from the bed.

My body feels all wrong, like my legs are made of jelly, and I can't take a firm step. But judging by the long moment it takes him to sit up, he's feeling it, too.

I hurry through the suite and finally swing open the

door. Brenda's standing there in mom jeans with her fist raised to continue knocking, a wide, hypercaffeinated smile on her face.

"Finally! You weren't answering your phone, and . . ."

She trails off, head tilting to the side, her high ponytail falling to the right as she eyes me up and down.

"I—it was on silent mode," I reply, my throat dry.

I stand there like I'm petrified while Brenda wanders around me. "Why do you look weird . . . red in the cheeks . . . hmm . . ."

I clear my throat, and, of course, this is the moment William chooses to leave the bedroom and come meet us. Brenda grins wolfishly. William opens and closes his mouth.

"Good . . . morning?" he tries.

"Was it a good morning? I don't know, man. You tell me." Brenda raises her eyebrows, grin still in place. She turns to me. "*Was* it good?"

I'm going to kill Brenda.

Shut up! I mouth to her. My cheeks are burning, and I'm going to pass out at any second now. I sneak a peek at William.

He's biting back a smile, like I do sometimes. He looks so beautiful, and his hair is so fluffy and I want to smile at him forever.

When Brenda speaks again, she's laughing.

"Ooookay," she says. "Let's go have some breakfast, *fake* lovebirds. Padma's already downstairs with everyone."

"Um, right." William says. I read the question in his eyes: *Is she going to stay here and wait for us? We know where the breakfast room is!*

I widen my eyes back. *I know we know! But she's—it's okay she's waiting for us! It shows she cares! See how nice? She likes you!*

William sighs in frustration, then shakes his head slightly. His eyes say: *Shouldn't we talk? In private? About what has happened?*

I make a pouting face, then shrug. *I'm perfectly fine with Brenda's company here. What should we talk about? Breakfast? I don't see the need for any pre-breakfast conversation.*

There is a possibility he didn't *quite* get that entire eye conversation like I did, but he does turn away to get dressed, and I offer Brenda an awkward smile before grabbing some clothes and disappearing into the bathroom.

Chapter 22

Still Alive

As expected, the breakfast room is incredible. Crystal chandeliers grace a massive room with large windows overlooking the beach. It's full of life, all late teens and early twenty-somethings laughing and clinking their glasses of either orange juice or bottomless mimosas. Brenda has one arm linked through mine and one through William's as she guides us to Padma's table. I try not to laugh at the absurdity of it all.

"We're here!" Brenda yells, letting both of us go and melting when she sees her girlfriend. Padma spreads her arms, and Brenda promptly sits on her lap and hugs her neck. "Missed you!"

"They're so gushy it's disgusting," I murmur to William.

His lips quirk. I clear my throat, sit down, and gesture for him to take the seat next to mine.

We're getting some curious looks, but the hotel is expensive enough that this is probably not those people's first encounter with someone famous. I don't see any phones pointed our way, at least.

"Anyway, let's *eat*."

William gives me one last furtive glance before he orders pretty much everything on the menu for himself. While he's talking to the waiter, Padma, on my other side, elbows me and whispers, "Have you checked Twitter or Insta yet?"

I give her a sheepish smile. "No, but I saw the video last night. And the pics. The whole thing."

Padma parts her lips, but then William turns to me. "What would you like?"

"Um, some pineapple juice and scrambled eggs," I tell the waiter, and he nods.

William bumps his shoulder to mine, apparently for no specific reason.

My face is hot.

I like how close we're sitting.

While Brenda entertains William, Padma elbows me again, this time gesturing so I can see her phone screen. I glance down. It's a thread called WHY TRENTALIE IS STILL ALIVE. I shoot her a confused look and scroll through. The first few items are garbage, like him following me on social again, but eventually I stop at a recent post. It has two pictures of Trent meeting fans in the Faro airport.

The caption reads: HE WENT ALL THE WAY TO PORTU-
GAL TO GET HIS GIRL.

My heart stops. I shoot a wide-eyed look at Padma.

She locks her phone and puts it back on the table, face-
down.

"I can't believe you've seen that film!" William smiles
at Brenda. "Isn't it brilliant? I love the direction they took
with making *Hamlet* a horror story. When you think about
it, isn't it the way it's supposed to be?"

"A nerdy take, but I agree," Brenda says.

I turn to Padma, whispering, "What the hell?"

Padma makes a face, then shakes her head. "I don't
know. He must've seen the pictures from the festival and
hated that your relationship is getting more publicity."

My stomach sinks. I can't believe this is happening.

I shut my eyes.

"Merda," I curse.

William turns to me with a question in his eyes, but he
never gets to ask. His eyes shift past me, to someone else.

And I know exactly who it is.

Chapter 23

I Am Her Boyfriend

*I*f I close my eyes long enough, can I make it all disappear?

I'm telling my empty stomach to settle down and not get any crazy ideas when *he* stops behind me. I can feel his looming presence, but he doesn't give me the option of ignoring him.

"Natalie," Trent says. "We need to talk."

Now I can see the phones pointed toward us even as I try not to. The whole room is paying attention, not only the people at my table.

I turn around to face him, but I'm still sitting. He's taller than I remember. His hair is a little longer. "I don't want to talk to you, Trent. I told you this before."

"I don't know why you think you have the right to her

time," Brenda says. Padma murmurs her name, and Brenda scoffs. "Just saying."

Trent's eyes pause on Brenda for a millisecond before they're back on me. "Anyway, as I was saying . . . I think, as your boyfriend, I deserve to talk to you in private."

I am so outraged I can't find the words. How can he be so deluded?!

Brenda scoffs again, and I have the feeling Padma is getting ready to physically restrain her, but it's not her reaction that catches my eye this time. It's William, frowning, his voice firm as he asks, "Excuse me? As her *what*?"

"I am her boyfriend," Trent says, towering over us. "And I've got a bunch of Twitter threads to prove it. You're just a placeholder."

It's the first time I see William properly angry. I could swear his green eyes turn icy when he narrows them, fists balled, ready for a fight that I know he won't start. I can't even breathe properly—I'm too preoccupied with all the cell phones in our direction.

"Don't worry about keeping up a front, dude. You're not really dating. Some random person heard you talk about how it's fake somewhere? I don't know. You're someone she paid to go out with so the public would stop talking about her People's Choice faux pas."

I hate the way he says *faux pas,* pronouncing the *x* and the *s* like a loser. I hate that he's staring at William like he's superior to him. I hate that he said he's my boyfriend. I hate that he thinks he can still cash in on me. I hate him so much.

William glances at me. "Nati?"

I don't know what to tell Trent, is the thing. Technically, he *is* right. William and I are fake-dating.

Or maybe he *was* right? After this morning, it feels like the game has changed.

"The *faux pas* that *you* caused, asshole," Brenda snarls at him.

Trent full-on ignores Brenda, and snorts at William instead. "It's *Natalie*," he corrects.

William tilts his chin up. "Is it now?"

There's a second there where they stare at each other, and I want to scream.

Then Trent gives up on the staring contest and turns to me. "Let's go, babe. We have a lot of talking to do."

"*Babe*?! What—" I stop myself. "Go away, Trent."

William glances at me.

"Two minutes. It's all I'm asking. If you don't like what I have to say, I'll leave you and your friends alone."

I cover my face with my hands and sigh.

I'm so done feeling like this is somehow my fault.

"I have to," I say, turning to William. "I need to get some things off my chest."

William parts his lips.

"Some bad things," I clarify.

I don't wait for him to respond. I'm already up and gesturing to the lobby, acting against every intuition in my being. As I walk, Trent puts his hand on the small of my back. I slap it away, and he doesn't try again. I don't look back to see whether William noticed or not.

The lobby is loud and full of people coming and going, but it's better than the breakfast room with so many people filming.

I cross my arms and face Trent head-on. "What you did was unforgivable. And I'm not going to somehow try and forgive you. I'm not. You don't deserve it, and I don't deserve to pretend like it didn't happen, either. It did. You dumped and humiliated me publicly."

Trent raises his hand up for me to stop. "That's—that's not what happened. I never wanted for the camera crew to show up."

"No, no. I believe you." I give him a half smile. "You wanted to dump me minutes before my award. Which you knew I was both nervous and excited for, but you didn't care. Because you never really cared about me, Trent. I don't think you're even capable of caring about someone who's not . . . you."

He shakes his head indignantly. "That's not fair. Plus . . . I came all this way to tell you"—he takes a deep breath—"that I'm sorry. I messed up, babe. Hey, I'm apologizing."

I look him up and down.

I can't believe I spent so many months with him. Incredible how low my bar was.

"Good. You should apologize. But I don't accept. I don't have to, and I don't want to."

Trent seems to be processing this. Then something must click for him, or he remembers the script he's planned. He smiles his stupid, fake smile. I never noticed before how much he looks like a shark.

"Anyway . . . whatever you say. But I see what you did, paying someone to follow you around, all to get my attention. It's cute. You got it. You have my full attention."

Closing my eyes seems like the best thing to do. I want to slap him, but that would make me the villain.

He continues as if he's received nothing but positive feedback from me. "So I decided to break up with Reese. She would've never done all the things you've done for me. Like, actually hiring someone to pretend to be your boyfriend so I'd be jealous? That's . . . that's romantic."

I open my eyes and stare at him with a cocked eyebrow.

"That's not romantic, Trent."

He comes a step closer to me. "Hey, I'm not judging."

More sharp teeth. God, he's gross.

"And it's not what happened, either." I press my lips together, scanning him for something lovable. He's attractive, but he's a copy of a copy of a copy.

There's nothing remarkable about him. No curly hair,

no crooked nose, no birthmark on his cheek, no funny socks, no bright smirk or weird sense of humor. Trent is plain. Bleak. He's nothing.

"You're still in love with me, Natalie. Quit playing games." He comes closer still, putting a hand on my arm.

I'm physically repulsed. It's an involuntary action, like someone hitting your knee and it jerking forward. I immediately take a step back, staying out of his personal space, staying away from his touch.

"Don't," I say.

If he hears me, he doesn't *listen*. And come to think of it, throughout those eight months, he never listened. It was me talking into the void, and Trent thinking only of himself and his career.

I must've been an incredible stepping-stone for him.

Without warning, he grips my arm and pulls me closer. I put up my hands to push him away when he swoops in and crushes his lips against mine.

It isn't romantic. It isn't tentative. It's possessive and it's definitely without my consent.

It takes me a second to break out of the shock of it, though.

When I do, I see William.

He's standing with Brenda and Padma a few feet away, where the restaurant meets the lobby. Brenda has a hand on his arm, but when he looks at me and I look at him, something breaks.

He blinks, like he's swallowed something vile, nods at me in acknowledgment and starts toward the elevators. Brenda runs after him.

I turn to run after him too, but Trent is still gripping my arm. "Babe?"

"Oh my God, you dick!" I yell at Trent, not worrying this time about the possible scene I'm causing. Not worrying if anyone takes pictures or makes videos of this. "If you've ruined this for me, I'm going to hunt you down and end you where it hurts the most: your pathetic career." I point my index finger at his face, and then turn away.

His hand tightens painfully on my arm.

Padma raises her phone toward his face. "Say cheese and we'll have a cute video of another white boy who can't take no for an answer, and I bet even your fans won't defend you when this comes out." She smiles, a dangerous glint in her eye.

Trent pauses.

He removes his hand from my arm and takes a step back.

"I didn't—I've never. I would never."

Padma narrows her eyes. "Right." Then she turns to me. "Go get him, girl. I'll stay with the douche and make sure he doesn't cause any more harm."

I nod to her.

I have the greatest friends in the world.

I'm jogging up to the elevator when five tweens come

up at me. "Oh my God, it's Natalie!" one of them says in a high-pitched voice. The elevator doors slide open. "I *love* your music. Can we take a selfie?"

Stupid music career. That I love with all my heart but—

I nod, spreading my arms so they'll get in there as quickly as possible.

The elevator doors close.

The girls take a while to decide how they want to pose, and I suspect my face is a little more desperate in each one of the seemingly three hundred selfies they take. One of them says, "Your hair is different. Is that your natural hair?"

I touch it, and only then I remember that it's my natural curls.

I nod, a bit absentmindedly, shooting the elevator another apprehensively look.

"That's so fierce," one of the girls says. "Are you going to wear it like that now?"

I give her a warm smile. "Maybe. Girls, it's—it's been lovely to meet you, but I really have to go, okay?"

They agree, but it's too late—others have noticed, and they all head toward me. A mob of teens around my age comes this time, and it's more than I can count. They start approaching me, some more decidedly than others, asking for selfies and autographs and lives for their friends. I turn around, and Padma is giving Trent a mouthful. He looks paler than usual. I turn back to the elevator, but it doesn't magically bring William back.

"Natalie, Natalie!" calls a girl half my age, with crooked teeth and a bright smile.

I don't want to be rude. I can't afford to. Hasn't all of this been about saving my image? But my heart's starting to race far too fast. I need my asthma pump. I need to feel safe. Smile, smile, smile, and keep breathing. Inhale for four seconds, hold for seven, let go for eight.

Trapped in a small mob of fans who only mean well, I watch the elevator doors in a state of semi-panic. They open and close twice more, and then, on the third time, William emerges.

His eyes lock with mine mid-selfie. I part my lips, but something changes in the way he looks at me. It's like bitter acceptance. Like he's making up his mind about me.

I try to call out his name, but I can't get any air into my lungs.

He leaves.

"That selfie doesn't look good. You looked away! Can we take another one?"

Why can't I make my feet move? He's leaving. He's leaving *me*.

I can't breathe, I can't breathe.

Just smile. Take another selfie.

"Yes! This looks perfect."

I don't know how much time later—a few seconds? Minutes? A whole quarter of an hour?—Padma and Brenda both come to my rescue. I feel Brenda's protective arms around me, pulling me away from the fans, and Padma flashes them her most charming smile and says that I'm needed somewhere else. The fans quickly get excited about DJ Lotus, and she takes my place.

"Brenda, I—" I turn to her, still lost. Numb. "I lost him."

She says something I don't quite get, and then her arms are around me. I'm still seeing white around the corners of my vision, my lungs still burning. I hear her voice echo in my head, *Breathe, Natalie. Just breathe.*

"Nati," I correct her, my own voice sounding choked up and far away.

I'm not sufficiently *there* to see her reaction, but I do hear her calling my name another time, instructing me to keep breathing. So I do. I breathe in for four seconds, hold for seven seconds, and let go for eight. My head is pounding but my vision eases. I blink at her, and she lets go of the embrace. There's a little smile in the corner of her mouth, and then Padma arrives, no evidence of Trent.

"What did I miss?" she asks.

"It's Nati now," Brenda says. I think this smile means she's proud.

I nod slowly. More composed now, I clear my throat, my eyes trail after the exit.

Brenda adds, "Go get him."

Chapter 24

A Guy Like That

"Where are we going, lady?" the cabdriver asks, idling outside the hotel.

"Just wait a little bit longer, please. He'll answer."

> **NATALIE:**
>
> where are you?????
>
> we need to talk

"Why don't you call him?"

I narrow my eyes. Okay, so maybe the driver isn't entirely against this happening. I lower my eyes to my phone and pause when my thumb's about to hit his name. What am I going to say? I purse my lips.

For better or for worse . . . I press call, and it starts ringing.

The cabdriver sighs heavily.

I cover my mouth with one hand, the other pressing the phone so hard against my face that my ear grows hot. My legs start going up and down, up and down, up and down....

Damn it. I wish I'd brought my inhaler to Portugal.

"He's not picking up," I say, more to myself than the driver. "He's not picking up."

The guy shoots me a look through the rearview mirror and says, "We can go to the airport. That's where everyone goes when they leave this hotel." He shrugs and deliberately checks his watch.

The call goes to voicemail. I end it.

"The airport..." I'm still holding my phone. "That isn't a bad idea."

Though it is, kind of, because the idea of William leaving without saying goodbye *hurts*. But I bet it also hurt to see Trent kiss me.

I groan, throwing my head back against the pleather seat of his cab.

"Miss?" he insists. "If you're sitting there, we have to go somewhere. This is my job."

I nod, murmuring, "Okay. Let's go."

> **NATALIE:**
>
> i'm going to the airport

I keep staring at my phone screen until it goes dark. I keep waiting for him to text me back or call. The twenty-minute drive to the airport is torturous. Eventually, I put the phone back in my purse. My bag is still at the hotel; Brenda did say that they'd take it back to Los Angeles if need be, but . . .

God, please make it *not* needed.

I hope Trent rots. It gives me certain pleasure to know that his acting skills are C+ at best, and that he's only getting by because of his looks.

His looks will end. His personality will sadly last forever.

The driver pulls onto the freeway, and as I take in the busy traffic on both sides of the road, I'm cursing Faro. Why does its airport have to be so far away from everything?

"Are you all right, miss?" the driver asks.

I ponder telling him my life story, but instead I go with "Fine."

"You seemed like you were going to have a heart attack back there." He chuckles. "Don't worry. A guy like that isn't going to go very far."

I frown, nearly strangling myself in the seat belt as I try to get closer to the driver seat. "What do you mean, 'a guy like that'? Did you see him? William?"

"Nah, but I mean, they're all the same." He shrugs, eyes ahead. "Any guy that comes from that hotel isn't going to get very far in the FAO."

I scrunch up my nose. "FAO? What?" And then, a little offended, "I'll have you know that William isn't *the same*. Certainly not the same as Trent. He's different. He's . . ." I breathe out heavily. "Why did he have to leave?"

The guy gives me a concerned look through the rear-view mirror.

"FAO is the airport. Faro Airport. I have no idea who William or Trent are, lady. I'm just saying people that stay in that hotel come from money, and unless your boyfriend is flying low-cost, there's no way he's leaving that airport for a long time."

My eyes widen. My heart skips a beat.

"Oh, he's *definitely* flying low-cost! Please, go faster!"

I slide back on my seat and murmur to myself, "I can't lose him."

Finally, my phone beeps. My heart races.

It's him.

No, no, no.

As we pull into the departures drop-off lane, the driver wishes me luck on my *romantic pursuits,* and I'm out of the cab as fast as humanly possible. I rush into the airport trying to find the screen with departure times, looking around to see if I can spot William's head of brown curls in the meantime. I hear a soft camera click here and there, maybe one or two fans who recognize me, but I'm trying not to pay attention to them, either.

Snap as many pictures as you want. No makeup, no hair done, no filter.

My phone buzzes again, and my heart warms when I see that it's William calling. I take a deep breath for good luck and answer.

"William," I say. "Listen, you have to let me explain."

On the other end, William sighs. "I have to tell you somethin—"

I pause in front of the departures board, scanning it for the next flight to London. Cutting him off, I add, "No, please. Please don't go. You have to let me explain."

"This is so difficult...." He trails off, letting out a bitter laugh. "Hearing your voice makes it all so much more difficult. But I really do have to leave."

I'm holding the phone so hard that my knuckles are turning white.

Breathe in. Breathe out.

There are no planes leaving for London right now, so he has to be somewhere near. I look around, frantic, only letting him speak for a few seconds as I search for him. "No, look, please, I'm here, come talk to me."

"Actually, Nati, I—" he starts, but I cut him off again.

Hearing him say my name like this...

"I don't want Trent. He's irrelevant. I don't want you to think—I care about *you*. He kissed me, and I didn't kiss him back! I didn't want to—I don't want to be with him. I want to be with you."

He's silent on the other end for a few seconds.

"I figured. The kiss shocked me at first, but I figured... And I do care about you, too, it's not..." He tsks. "I care about you so much. But I can't do this. I have to go home. I have to go back to my world."

My brow furrows. "You still think about it as my world and your world, as if I'm a princess and you're a commoner or something? Well, guess what, William? You're in the biz, too! And it's okay if you prefer to keep it low-key and focus on the art. Because you're . . ." I sigh. "You're pretty wonderful the way you are. But don't say *your* world and *my* world. I'm just . . . I'm just trying to find my place in *this* world."

He breathes out softly on the other end.

To his benefit, he sounds as shattered and broken as I feel.

"I'm sorry, Nati. I . . . need some space. I need to think."

"William," I plead, almost a whine. Because I opened my heart to him. And this isn't fair. I want things to go back to the way they were. Fake boyfriend minus the fake part. *"Why?"*

"Because!" he says, the exasperation clear in his voice. I cling to the phone, I hold my breath and close my eyes. Anything to keep this moment from being real. "I was trying not to think about it, trying to live in the moment with you, but . . . Trent is an arse, but that big scene at the hotel? Everyone recording it and elbowing one another? That's . . . your life. And it isn't the life I want for myself. I can't live a life with no privacy, putting my family at risk, can't put on a smile like that, like you can." He takes a deep breath, and I wince. "And I guess I signed up for it. But it was because I thought I wouldn't care. I thought it wouldn't make a difference to me . . . but it does. And I can't do this."

"But . . ." I have nothing else to say.

He's heard me.

It didn't make a difference.

"I've been trying to tell you—I'm not at the airport. I'm at the train station, and my train is about to leave. Good-bye, Nati."

Click. The call is over.

It's all over.

Chapter 25

From the Beginning, It Was You

I refuse to cry in public *again*.

Sitting down in a café, I focus on people-watching, which is the only thing that makes me feel a little less unmoored, a little less like my mind's going around and around without reaching a destination.

I lower my head, taking a sip of my cappuccino, and unlock my phone. I made him my lock screen. Shouldn't that mean something?

I open the Notes app and start drafting *something*. Not quite a song, I don't think. But maybe the seeds of one. I pour out my frustration and my loneliness, and the feeling that I have to constantly prove myself to belong. Prove that I deserve to be here, deserve to be heard. I pour out my feelings for William, and falling for his kindness and gentleness, and being on alert mode for signs of Trent in him, even though that never came.

It's the last few months in lyric format.

When I'm done with the brainstorm of too many words and no melody, I read through it. The person I want to send it to is William. But I can't call and I can't text, so I open Instagram instead.

His account . . . is no longer active.

This has to be a mistake.

I open Twitter. No longer active.

"No, no, no," I whisper.

A woman in a business suit is sitting at the next table. She adjusts her laptop and glares at me. I glare back. C'mon, lady. I'm not even being loud. Just let me sit in despair by myself. Or . . . maybe I don't have to?

I call Mom. She answers on the first ring.

"Filha? Everything okay?"

I breathe out as long and loud as I can. Not to upset the lady who's already upset. Because I have to. "So far from okay. I . . . I don't know what to do, Mom. William left. He's going back to London. And I can't make him stay. And Trent came here and kissed me, which, *gross.* But that's what triggered it for William, I think. He's not upset with me, he's . . . I think he's upset with everything around us. And I don't know how to make that stop, Mom. I don't know how to make him know that it's okay and there's no *my* world and *his* world. I don't know what to do."

She doesn't ask when William started to matter so much. She doesn't ask about Trent. She doesn't ask anything.

She listens, and then sighs.

When she speaks, her voice is quiet and loving and feels like a hug, even if it stings. "If he wants to go, there's nothing you can do, filha. You have to let him go."

With my free hand, I grip my cappuccino.

"But—"

I don't have any real arguments. I know she's right.

She's Mom.

Brazilian moms are always right.

I look down at my drink, my other hand pressing the phone so hard against my ear that it hurts. I try to breathe out this frustration, this . . .

"Natalia," Mom starts, then pauses for a second. "You can come home, too."

There's this knot in my throat. It's always there. I've learned to ignore it over the years, but at times like this, it becomes impossible. I shift in my seat, looking down, suddenly feeling like there's an anvil on my chest.

"I know you don't miss him . . . ," I start, then clear my throat so my voice doesn't sound as strangled. "I'm sorry, you don't know what I'm talking about—I mean my father. I know you don't miss him. I don't miss him, either. I mean, *what* would I miss?" I snort. She's quiet on the other end.

"But I miss the idea of a dad, I guess? Do you ever get angry at him for leaving?"

Mom sighs softly. "Sometimes. Mostly because of you." I can hear the loving smile in her voice. "He didn't deserve you—"

"I do get angry." I cut her off, and she lets me get away with it for once. "I don't want you to think that it's . . . a thing. It's not. I don't think about him. But every now and then, I remember I know what it's like to be abandoned, and I really hate Dad for showing me what that's like."

"Meu amor," she says. I hear moving, and then she says, "It's his loss. I am so proud of the woman you're becoming. I am so happy that I got to live through all your birthdays and Christmas Eves, every time you had a sore throat or a cold, and when you learned to speak and read and sing."

I chuckle lowly, feeling the need to lighten the mood. "It's funny that you didn't mention my world tours or awards."

"Is it really? You know me better than that."

"I do," I admit. "And I'm proud of you, too, Mom. I love you so much. Te amo."

We're quiet for another moment. I don't know what's on her mind, but I know I'm letting it all sink in. Because it *is* my father's loss. And I meant it when I said I don't think about him much at all.

My father is a dick. I don't think I'd want him in my life either way.

William isn't. And I very much do want him in my life.

"I'm at the airport," I say, starting over. "I was waiting for William, but he isn't coming. He deleted all his social media."

Mom doesn't have social media, so I hardly expect her to understand what it means to go MIA like this. For me, I'd be making a pretty big statement by saying nothing. It would mean disappearing.

But she knows me well enough to predict what's going on in my mind.

"He's not you," she tells me. "Maybe he needs a break from living under a microscope."

I bite the insides of my mouth. I stare down at the table as if it were the most amazing piece of art I've ever seen.

"That's worse. Because then it means he'll never want to be with me."

Mom doesn't immediately respond. "William's an artist, too, isn't he? I didn't say he'd *never* want to join you again under the microscope."

I force myself to relax. It doesn't work very well—my shoulders are still stiff—but at least it doesn't feel like I can only speak through a clenched jaw anymore.

"But not like me," I say. "Everyone's always speculating about what I'm doing. Everyone's always posting pictures. Everyone's always watching me. Wherever I go, I just . . ." I trail off, looking to the side. As if on cue, two girls holding hands take the table where the woman was sitting before.

They're both gawking at me. "What if he tried the spotlight long enough for fake that he realized he doesn't want it for real?"

"Oh, baby," she states matter-of-factly, as if that's it. That's the answer. But the real answer takes another moment. She says it lovingly, which makes it sting all the more. "Then you'll *really* have to let him go."

I can feel all the breath leaving my lungs in one big whoosh, like a balloon deflating.

"Maybe he needs a moment to figure out where he stands, and figure out his own feelings. Weren't you under contract until a hot minute ago?" she asks.

"We still are, technically." The idea of *making* him come back rises and then dies in its absurdity a second later. I groan and try to see a way out, but I don't know what else to say, either.

This isn't how it was supposed to go. I was supposed to fight for him. Fight for us to go from fake to real. I was supposed to rush to the airport and announce that he was wrong and I was right. That we . . . that we belong together. Win him back.

Weird socks and all.

Instead he's on a train, and I'm in this café, saying goodbye to Mom and thanking her for listening, because there's still a part of me who wants to believe all her advice means nothing. That I won't have to let him go.

I finish my cappuccino. I ask for another. I hold the cup

with both hands to warm my palms and wonder if there's any use going over my feeds, reading the conspiracy theories about why William deleted his social media. But there'd probably be too much of Trent in those, and if I never see his face again, it'll be too soon.

I run my hands over my hair, and it's a strange reminder that it's curly, not straight. I had forgotten. I'm not wearing any makeup, either. Has someone taken a picture? Has someone already uploaded it and called my natural hair a natural disaster? That I've lost both boys the internet shipped me with, and thus I'm sporting a new, hopeless look?

The thought makes me snort. I let my eyes roam, and they find the girls who walked in during my phone call. They're still watching me, but this time, when I glance their way, they look at each other, alarmed, as if they'd been caught doing something terrible.

They're younger than me. Probably fourteen? I remember that acne stage way too well. I was already performing, which means I had to get very comfortable with lots of concealer.

I glance their way again.

One of them is brown, with round eyes and braids. The other is white, with thin blond hair and a T-shirt that says GIRLS LIKE GIRLS. They don't have any luggage with them.

They notice my gaze, and after a whispered conversation, they reluctantly come my way. They stand before me, holding hands, like a barrier of excited fan love.

What a ridiculous thought. Why would they feel this powerful finding me in shreds in an airport? They don't even have their phones in hand.

Not here for a selfie, then.

"I'm Carla, and this is Betina," the girl with braids says. "And you're *Natalie*."

Her accent is thickly Brazilian. The way she says my name, Americanized, I hate it.

It makes me want to cry.

"I . . . am?" I offer, trying to smile.

Betina says, "We are your biggest fans! We can't wait for you to perform in Brazil!" She chuckles, looking at Carla, and their shoulders go up in a shrug at the same time, in a cute and ridiculously synced moment. "We live in Ceará, but we'd totally travel to São Paulo or Rio for you. You know, if you come."

The other girl, Carla, talks to her in Portuguese, "Cuida o que você fala! Vai parecer que tá exigindo. Ela pode ficar chateada."

I get enough of that to know that (a) Carla is worried Betina will come off as demanding, and I'll be upset about that, and (b) neither of them has any idea that *I* have any clue about Portuguese.

I shrink in my seat.

"Thanks for following me, girls. Your support means a lot to me." I smile.

It's a genuine smile. A sad one, but genuine. I feel like I owe them this much.

They stand before me for a moment longer, as if they're practicing what to say in their heads. Then Carla says, "We don't want to bother you. We really don't. And we know that you, as an international artist, would never do a tour around Brazil or anything; we wouldn't *expect* someone as awesome and popular as you to spend more than a few days, but we really would go to the biggest cities for you. It would mean so much for us to see you sing."

She's tearing up.

Oh God.

I've made a girl cry.

My eyes widen and I start to stand up, then sit back down. She picks up on my panic, because she wipes her eyes with the backs of her hands. "It's okay! I'm just emotional."

I press my lips together.

I feel ashamed that I didn't want to return home for the holidays. I feel ashamed that I haven't returned in years. My stomach sinks.

"I sang your song 'From the Beginning, It Was You' to her when I asked her to be my girlfriend." Betina grins from ear to ear. I bring my hands to my chest, truly touched by that. I wrote "From The Beginning, It Was You" in the beginning of my career. I wanted to fall in love. I wanted connection. Most of all, I wanted to be singing this to someone who'd make me feel larger than life. Someone who'd make me feel invincible. But the chance never came.

"Basically, we love you!" Betina continues. "And it means so much to us to have you out there, kicking ass, getting all the awards. . . ."

Carla sniffs. "They don't see a lot of value in us. Europeans. Americans." She shrugs, a shadow passing her face. "We're more fortunate than most; we get to travel sometimes with Betina's mom, because she's a flight attendant. And then be treated poorly in many, many languages . . ."

I notice Betina squeeze her hand.

There's a knot in my throat.

"But you are changing the game," Betina says. "My sister talks all the time about how she'd never thought she'd see a Brazilian praised worldwide. Here you are, living your truth, and making sure everyone knows how great you are."

My eyes blur.

The thing that's beaming from them? That's pride. They're proud of me.

I study these two girls. Their brightness. Their strength.

"Thank you," I tell them. "*You* are really great, and I'm so proud of you for living your truth . . . it's inspiring. You have inspired me. That's what I wanted to say." I take a deep breath. "Listen, I . . . I'll do a Brazilian tour. I have to talk to my agent about the details, but—but I'll do it. I really, really want to."

Their expressions change. They look at each other as if they've been given a precious gift. It makes me want to cry all over again, watching them like this.

I mean it, about the tour. I will make it happen.

"That would mean so much," Betina says, choked up.

I'm choked up, too. I only nod in appreciation.

They say goodbye, smiling from ear to ear. They leave the café without having ordered anything.

I swallow the knot in my throat.

I leave some extra euros of tip on top of the table and grab my bag. I can't be late; I have a flight to catch, and I still have to buy the ticket. On my way there, I type a message to William.

> **NATALIE:**
>
> i guess sometimes it takes time. when you're ready, i'm here.

I stare at the message for a long moment. Something in my chest tightens, and I go to the phone settings. Once I'm there, I change the last letter in my name, from *Natalie* to *Natalia*.

From something I'm not to something I've always been.

Chapter 26

The Death of Natalie

"*I* think both of you know why I'm standing here in front of you," I tell Bobbi and Ashley with an ear-to-ear grin.

We're not in Bobbi's office. We're in her conference room, in front of the PowerPoint screen. The room is so much bigger and brighter—almost a surgery room. Which is fitting enough. We're about to perform a serious operation.

Ashley studies me with her best poker face. Bobbi, though, I can tell that she's puzzled.

"I was hoping you'd start by explaining that, after all, it's been *quiet* on your end," Bobbi starts, then turns to Ashley. "Where's Ainsley?"

"London, apparently," Ashley replies, frowning slightly. "But I will contact his manager. We can stage a PR outing that will be—"

I interrupt them both, clearing my throat loudly. "I—that won't be necessary. Um." Take a deep breath in, a long breath out. I got this. "Well, first, I'd like to politely decline the invitation to buy a pre-written album." I scan the room for reactions, but their faces stay the same. "And . . . I made a PowerPoint presentation in case you weren't following social media." I turn on the projector and off the lights.

While I'm busy doing that, Ashley announces, "It's borderline offensive that you accuse a PR specialist of not following social media. Of course I've been following social media. Closely. For all of my clients. And I follow you closely enough to know that you haven't been posting anything for two weeks, since the Faro festival with DJ Lotus and William Ainsley. Nada. It's like you—"

She stops herself, but I know what she wants to say: *It's like you* want *to be forgotten.*

I clear my throat and point at the dark screen in front of us.

"Are you ready for my presentation?"

Each of them stares. Ashley with that unblinking expression of hers, Bobbi with a rather concerned look.

I put on my brightest smile and click next on the projector controller. An all-black screen with the text THE DEATH OF NATALIE appears. I don't focus on their reactions, but instead start talking. "I want to rebrand." I pace the room with the controller in hand. "You may have noticed that my hair isn't straightened. These curls? Natural. The makeup I'm wearing? Minimal—"

Bobbi cuts me off. "Do you really want to send the message to your fans that girls can't wear makeup? Femininity can be empowering."

Ashley cocks an eyebrow. "Makeup isn't exclusively feminine. And femininity is just one way of empowerment, not by any means the only."

I clear my throat, impressed by Ashley. "I'm not going to tell anyone not to wear makeup. Anyone who wants to do it should do it. I'm doing it. But I don't want to go through *so much* to look perfect. If I have a zit, I'm going to show up with a zit."

Bobbi tsks. "Surely not if you're performing?"

I open and close my mouth. Then I nod. "I guess, if I'm performing, I need enough makeup so the lights won't make me look dead." Bobbi nods back at me, still a little concerned.

"This is me as a kid." I press next, and pictures of me after I came to the United States pop up on the screen. In one picture, I'm on the couch, sticking out my tongue, with a Brazilian flag wrapped around me like a blanket.

"I realized I lost someone very, very dear to me." I turn to the screen again. "I lost *her*. But with your help, I can get her back."

"What do you think?" Bobbi asks Ashley. "Could you

revamp her image to something closer to this more natural Natalie? Maybe next year?"

Ashley's about to respond when I step into the conversation, shaking my head, a little knot in my throat. "No, no, no. First, this has to be now. I'm ready. And second . . . it's not Natalie anymore. It's Nati."

"Nati?" Ashley repeats, with a strong T.

I shake my head again. "Nah-tchy."

She narrows her eyes. "People are going to have trouble pronouncing it. They'll miswrite it. They'll hear you on the radio, then want to stream your albums and not find you because they can't get your name right."

I cross my arms over my chest, raising an eyebrow.

"If I've learned to pronounce *Gwyneth* and *Sean,* and spell *Kathryn, Katherine, Catherine,* and so on in a thousand different ways, you can learn my name."

They look at each other. Perhaps my point wasn't really made without a visual of the three spelling variations. I shake my head, going back to the presentation and pressing to the next slide. The screen turns white, with a list of six titles.

After two weeks of intense scrutinizing of my Notes app for lyrics and working on new ones, I'm finally ready. It's the most I've worked in such a short period of time, but I'm proud of the preliminary results. I'm proud of every moment of confession that's turned into flowing lyrics. I'm excited to hit the studio and give it all the love these new songs deserve.

"I've written them over the past couple weeks. I'm ready to start recording."

"Whoa!" Bobbi smiles, then applauds. "This is going to be a great way to start the new year. I'm so proud of you for managing to write so much in such a short time."

I run my hand over my curls, taking the deepest breath I've taken in the past few weeks. "This has to be now. I even wrote a Christmas song!" I point at track 3: "Natal at Home," the song I wrote about my family, my insecurities and fears, and as a way of celebrating them, too. "Listen, I know it's short notice. I know it's only two weeks until Christmas. And everyone is booked for Christmas events months in advance," I add, before Bobbi can. She hums in acknowledgment. "But I need you to give me something. Pull your strings, Ashley, I know you have many. You've come through for me when everyone was making memes of me, making fun of my breakup with Trent. I need you to come through for me one more time."

She stays silent. I'm seconds away from begging.

"Why now?" Bobbi asks, sounding genuinely curious.

"Because now I'm ready," I tell her.

"This won't do," Ashley announces, shaking her head.

My heart sinks.

But I made a presentation!

I need her. I can't do this alone. Even if Bobbi tries to call every single network and person hosting an event, she won't have as much reach as she would with Ashley by her side.

Please.

She breathes out, sitting back. "'The Death of Natalie' is a terrible name. What was that even supposed to be? Your new album?" she asks.

I turn back to the presentation and nod.

"No, that won't do. If we're relaunching your image and making everyone learn to call you by your Brazilian nickname, we're going to need a much stronger album title. A much stronger concept."

I can feel my pulse quickening, this time in anticipation. "Does this mean you're in?"

Ashley nods. "Yes. Yes, Nati, I am."

And she says it right.

Chapter 27

#WhereIsNati?

I've always loved the elevator to our apartment, because the all-around mirrors make it look like I'm part of a sci-fi movie, ready to save the world. I marvel at my half-curly, half-wavy hair, at how my face looks with a bit of mascara and a soft pink lipstick. I pull my dark hair to the side, exposing my ears and a pearl earring. I like what I see. Lately, I've been liking a lot of what I see when I step into this elevator.

My phone vibrates, and I take it out of my purse. It's from the girls group chat. They're sending selfies. I stick out my tongue and send one back.

I do what I always do when I grab my phone: I go to William's profiles and accounts. Still nonexistent. Something twists inside of me, but I push it aside.

As I go back to my feed, sure enough, there are fans

speculating about Trentalie being back. It doesn't make me feel bad anymore. I mostly pity Trent and feel like I wasted eight months of my life doing a lot of mental gymnastics to convince myself he was something he wasn't.

But if it hadn't been for our very public and humiliating breakup, I wouldn't have been desperate to fix my image. And I wouldn't have had a soft British boy on my arm.

I shake that thought away, too.

"Not the time, not the time," I say out loud, like a mantra.

But I keep scrolling through my feed, and eventually the hashtag I was really searching for appears: #WhereIs-Nati? I grin at that and click it. In it, fans and haters alike speculate on everything from my possible death and the existence of doppelgängers to a theory closer to the truth: that I'm going to drop a new album without any previous promo. My rebranding involved deleting all pictures from Instagram, all tweets from Twitter. My only hint is my pro-file picture, a purple background with the word NATI on it.

Bobbi believes the new album is going to do fine, that the lack of promo will be offset by the buildup from dis-appearing for a few weeks. I've already got the fanbase I need to make my album a chart-topping success. Beyoncé does it all the time.

Anyway, I'm not that focused on the sales. The fact that the fans have shifted from Natalie to Nati as soon as

I changed my social media handles and names is enough for now.

The doors slide open, and I start toward my apartment.

My key's halfway in the door when Mom opens it. "I thought I heard something!" She pulls me into a hug, so tight and sudden, that I'm perplexed, still holding the keys in one hand, my purse in the other.

My face squished against the crook of her neck, I say, "Good afternoon to you, too?"

Still holding me, she allows me some breathing room. She's smiling wide, beaming with pride, and I think I know what this is about. I smile, too.

"You weren't going to tell me, were you?" she teases.

I shrug. "I wanted it to be a surprise."

She rolls her eyes. "Eu dei a luz pra você, filha! Você não tem o direito de me esconder nada não." Her tone is still teasing. I know *filha* is "daughter." I know some of the verbs she used, but—"I said you have no right to hide anything from me, because I birthed you."

I make a face. "Okay?"

Mom motions me inside. "Bobbi called to say that they'd be ready for you if you wanted to start rehearsal today. I said that you've already been rehearsing day and night, and she told me that it's important you're at the top of your game in order to headline the Netflix Christmas special!"

She makes a face like she's going to burst.

"Yes!" I say, grinning. "Their headliner dropped out, and Bobbi managed to persuade them to make me the top performer!"

She takes me in her arms for a big bear hug again. I hug her back this time.

Mom pulls away, kisses both my cheeks, and holds my face. "I'm so proud of you, filha. This is so great. I can hardly believe it. I've already called Vovó, by the way. All the family is going to be watching you from Brazil as well."

"No pressure," I add, still smiling.

She tells me she'll bake some pão de queijo to celebrate, and I go to my room for a bit. I grab my guitar, scribble a few lyrics to look at later, but my mind keeps racing. I love this new era—just like I liked my old music, starstruck and innocent, and my most recent music, more independent and sure of myself. But this is different. More vulnerable, more open, ready to expose myself for the sake of a good song. I smile to myself and write down that thought as well. Not in lyric format yet, but I'm getting inundated by a flow of words lately.

I set the guitar and notebook aside on my bed, and take my phone. Then I scroll down for Vovó's number and call her. She picks up on the second ring. "Vovó? Oi, é a Nati. I wanted to know if . . . the invitation—convite! O convite pra passar o Natal com vocês. Is that still up? I mean, can I still come over for Christmas?"

Both Padma and Brenda are already at the café when I get there. I stand by the door for a second, taking them in. They look beautiful like this: Padma's arm draped over Brenda's shoulders, studying the menu as if she's about to make a life-changing decision.

If people knew the way they are with each other, they wouldn't waste their time getting invested in *my* relationships. They'd look at them instead.

Which makes me think . . . I miss William.

Not the status that would come with being his girlfriend. I miss his loud laughter and his mood-ring green eyes. I miss his sideway grin and weird socks.

I close the door behind me and make my way to the girls. When I drop my purse on the other side of the booth, Brenda jumps to greet me with a smile and a hug, and Padma reaches out her arms from where she's sitting.

"Too cold outside?" Padma asks, dropping her arms.

"LA cold." I shrug. Still, I take off my jacket. "Have you guys ordered anything?"

"Waiting for you," Brenda says. "But hot chocolate for all, right?"

"Right!" Padma and I say in unison, then laugh.

Brenda gets up. "I'll get it, then. My treat."

She winks on her way out, and I turn to her girlfriend. "What's up with her?"

Padma tilts her head at Brenda's abandoned phone on the table. "Guess who got accepted to Berkeley."

My jaw drops. I swallow down a scream of excitement, and when Brenda comes back, I play-slap her on the arm. "You're going to college! Oh my God! You're in!"

She laughs and nods, almost shy.

I've never seen Brenda look so timid before in my life.

"Congratulations, damn!" I slap the table, too, because I'm excited and full of feelings and I don't know how to speak without hurting people or things, apparently. "I mean, obviously I *knew* you'd get accepted anywhere you wanted—"

"Not true, I'm a very average student," Brenda interrupts, but I choose to ignore her.

"But still, getting that confirmation, gah!" I gesture like I'm going to grab her, then sit back on my side of the booth. "I'm really happy for you, B. You deserve this."

Padma slides her arm over Brenda's shoulders again, a proud smirk on her face.

"Yeah. She does."

I rest my chin on my hands, looking at them with a smile of my own.

"I just found out," Brenda takes her phone. "I was reading through some majors and stuff. I still don't know exactly what I'm going to major in, but that's—that's a thought for later, right?" she asks, scrolling down her phone attentively. "Here." She turns the phone to my face.

I can't really read the email because her hand is bouncing around, but the word *accepted* is in bold. I take her hand in mine. I don't know how to say it. We usually don't. She knows I'm there for her. I know she's there for me.

But this feels like one of those moments where you have to say something.

Brenda smiles back at me. "I know, Nati."

"I know you know. You're going to listen to it anyway, okay?" She's beaming. "I love you, Brenda." I grab Padma's hand even though she playfully tries to yank it away. "And I love you, too, Padma."

"We love you back," Padma replies, without an ounce of irony.

If the waiter hadn't come with our hot chocolates, I would have cried. Maybe.

But as he sets the drinks in front of each of us, we're still beaming. I take a sip of my hot chocolate to hide behind the large mug.

Padma says, "So I've seen Trent on my timeline, interacting with your fans."

I roll my eyes, putting the mug down. "Yeah, I saw that, too. He's making it sound like he knows what's going on, and is trying to get Trentalie fans to believe that we're back together. It's beyond pathetic. He's going to keep milking that cow until she runs dry. Still using me for fame even months after we've broken up."

"Are you the cow?" Brenda asks.

I flip her off with a smile.

Padma clears her throat awkwardly. I frown at her. *"What?"*

"How's that going, anyway?" she asks.

"How's what going?" But I know what she means.

Brenda takes a deep breath. "What's up with you and William?" Then she brings the drink to her lips, as if she's hiding behind it.

My eyes go down to my mug. I watch the warmth rise in a thin cloud. I press my palms against the glass.

"Nothing's up," I answer.

Padma snorts. "C'mon, Nati."

I shrug. "His social media is still dead. I guess there's nothing left to do. He chose not to be with someone like me and my fifty million followers."

"Show-off." Padma chuckles.

"I'm saying that it's overwhelming and smothering to have so many people flooding his social media saying that they either hate or love him with me, or talking about how much money he has, or I have," I say. "He never wanted that level of fame. He wants to do good movies he believes in. He wants . . . he wants to be an actor, but not to be super-famous. And you know what? I'm grateful for my fans, I really am. But it's not only them. It's the media. It's the tabloids. That's all . . . They're all valid reasons why he doesn't want me."

Padma's smile falters. She tries speaking, then stops.

On the second try, she says, "You're an amazing girl. If he doesn't want you for any reason at all, that's his loss. Plus it's not like you can do anything about it. You live in an aquarium. People watch you. It's part of the package."

"It's a lot to ask someone, to want in on the aquarium," I say, more to myself than her.

Padma doesn't tell me I'm wrong.

Brenda asks, "But he hasn't answered any of your texts? Total radio silence?"

"No, that'd be rude, wouldn't it?" Not that it really matters, because although our contract hasn't officially ended yet, we've pretty much agreed to end it. William owes me nothing, not even kindness. "He . . . he's not rude. He's answered, yeah. Said he was with his family, that they were all right. Even sent me a picture of his nephew playing. And on Hanukkah he sent me pictures of his sisters."

"Oh?" Brenda asks. "That . . . that may mean he still has feelings for you."

"He does," I answer, without skipping a beat. Then I add, "I . . . think. I hope. But whenever I write about him coming back, he stops replying. He's not ready for this. And I can't blame him." I shrug again.

There's a moment of silence. Not awkward, but punctuating the end of this talk. Maybe punctuating the end of all William-related talk? I know I don't want to talk about him. There's no point. It only hurts more.

"But I do have other news," I tell them. Brenda points

at the spot over her upper lip, and I look down, sticking out my lip until I can see a bit of chocolate. I lick it, and Padma lets out a disgusted noise. "Anyway, as I was saying, news!"

"Do tell," Brenda encourages.

"So, the Netflix special is in four days, but after that..." I trail off, trying to build on the suspense, and the two stare at me blankly. "I'm going to Brazil! I'm spending Christmas with my family. For the first time in years."

"Wow!" Brenda gasps, then covers her mouth.

Padma chuckles, nodding. "Nice, nice. Are you nervous?"

"Terrified," I admit. "But I have a good feeling about this, too."

Chapter 28

The Missing Piece

After six hours of intense recording, my producer looks like she might pass out. I, on the other hand, am ready to go all night. Which isn't mutually exclusive, since I assume I look just as rough.

Aline says, "Let's try it with a B minor," and her fingers slide across the keyboard as I hum the melody. We stare at each other. "No, that isn't it yet, is it?"

I fall on the couch of the small studio, putting my hands on my head. "I think we need a break."

Aline is wearing pink sneakers, Adidas sweatpants, and a T-shirt that says EVERYTHING IS BIGGER IN TEXAS. A lot less glamorous than her outfit at the premiere afterparty. Her hair is up in a bun as messy as mine, and she seems just as sleep-deprived. But it's the last song of the EP, and we both want it to be perfect.

She takes her glasses she'd forgotten on top of the keyboard and puts them back on. "All right. Let's go have some coffee in the reception. My treat," she jokes, and gives me a hand to help me up. We both know the coffee and snacks are free.

I offer her an apologetic smile. "You go ahead. I'm going to try to figure this out for a bit."

Aline rolls her eyes. "You said *we* need a break. Not that I need a break."

I try to come up with an excuse, but she holds up a hand to stop me with a hint of a smile.

"You know what? I was going to fake-pay for your coffee, but now I'm not in the mood anymore," she jokes. "When you decide to glow up, I'll be in the reception."

She waves goodbye and I'm left in the studio alone.

Fake-pay. Ha. *Fake* is a funny word.

. . . not ha-ha funny, exactly.

But no, I'm not going there. Right now, my focus is on my new album and this Netflix special, because after that, I'm announcing my South American tour and I need to be on top of my game.

And before that, before any of that, there's Christmas . . . which I *will* spend at home in Brazil, like the song says. At least that song's fully produced for the show in a few days.

Pulling my legs up, I straighten my purple-plaid T-shirt and baggy jeans, reading through what we've written so far. I make a face and grab the guitar, trying different combinations of the chords as I hum slowly. Have I found something? I try to sing along, but the lyrics don't match.

Head down, I'm focused on my work, but I hear the door open. Aline's already back, probably to bother me about taking a break. I'm still trying to make these strings sound the way it sounds in my head, so I don't look up.

"I can't take a break, Aline. After tonight, I'll be on vocal rest. I need to nail this down and record it tonight."

"That will be very hard if you burn out, won't it?"

My eyes widen.

Slowly, I look up.

It's not Aline. It's Gemma Santiago, holding two plastic cups of coffee, smiling at me.

Gemma Santiago, as in, the Latina icon who's topped the charts for the past decade. As in, my dream mentor. As in, the person who was supposed to give me my award before it all went to hell.

Gemma Santiago, walking to the couch to sit beside me.

I nearly drop my guitar but manage to set it aside as gently as possible. "Hi," I say, completely starstruck, even nine years after moving to Los Angeles.

"Hi," she responds good-naturedly. She's absolutely gorgeous, with her thick black curls and strong eyebrows, her dark brown skin and her round caramel eyes. She has freckles, like Mom, but I don't think most people see her without her makeup. "Bobbi mentioned you were hanging out at the studio, so I thought I'd check on how you were doing." She pauses, makes a face. "Hopefully it's not too late?"

I let out an embarrassing giggle.

She raises her eyebrows.

I clear my throat, trying to compose myself.

"I—thank you, I'm doing much better, yes. I . . . I'm finishing an EP, actually. It's going to be very different from what I've put out so far, but I'm excited about it." I smile from ear to ear, and she nods, like she understands. If anyone does, it's her. Speaking of which . . . "Actually, I have a question for you, if it's not too weird. A-are you okay? Are you . . . happy?"

God, what am I saying?

Seeing Gemma Santiago in normal clothes instead of her usual fancy dresses is wild. Jeans and a hoodie? Out of this world. I want to say words that make sense, but all I can think is, *Mom is going to freak when I tell her I've met Gemma Santiago.*

"Oh, love, who is happy all the time?" She laughs. "But generally happy, yes, I would say so." She takes a sip of her coffee. "Aline Hernandez is a great producer. You two will find the way to finish this song, don't worry. But you do have to cut yourself some slack. Breaks are important. If you don't have them, you're going to burn out. Now, what good can you do for your people if you're burned out?"

I like the way she says *my people*. I like the way she talks to me.

Trying to quiet the fangirl in my heart, I bite back a smile and take a sip from my coffee. "I think I want to do right."

"You will. You do. The fact that you're worried about it is half the battle." She raises her cup to mine, and we toast with them. "I'm sorry about what happened to you. It was a sad accident, and I'm deeply enraged about how people reacted to it. But that's people for you." Gemma lifts her shoulders, wrinkling her nose. "It's part of the business. If the good is enough to cancel out the bad, then we stay and do our best to change the status quo. And deal with what we can't change in the meantime."

I consider this.

"It *is* worth it for me," I confess. "I love that I get to do this. To write songs. Every bad or good thought I've had these past few months has become a song. I have a song for when you realize your boyfriend is not a good guy, and about self-proclaimed good guys. I have a song that transports me back to a phone call with my grandma when it hurt so much and I didn't understand why. I have a song for that specific moment when you kiss someone one morning and it feels like you've waited for that kiss your whole life. I have a song that hopefully encapsulates exactly what it feels like to be chasing the perfect guy when he's not ready yet."

Our relationship feels impossible to sum up, but I think I captured some of what I feel for William. Or what it feels like now, talking every day on the phone and FaceTiming each other until one of us falls asleep.

Trying to be friends, or something.

We do make a good pair of friends, if anything.

Even if I want to be so much more than that.

"But that thing you said . . . how you were enraged about the way people reacted to the memes and the things the tabloids said. I hadn't . . . I hadn't thought about it from that perspective." My brow furrows, and I glance at my guitar. "I know why this song isn't working. It's missing something."

Gemma blinks slowly. "What is it, Nati?"

"Justified anger," I reply. "Letting them know that if you're never going to be good enough for them, then you're going to be good enough for yourself and call it a day."

She narrows her big hazel eyes. "Sounds like good lyric-writing to me."

I take a deep breath and smile.

Gemma stands up, holding her coffee, and reaches out for a high five. I stand up, too, looking at her hand for a second, and then go for a hug instead. She receives me with open arms—or an open one-arm hug, still holding her coffee with the other hand.

"Ay, cariño. Cree en ti misma. Eres tan hermosa." She kisses my cheek.

I stand back. "I'm sorry, but I don't really speak Spanish."

She laughs. "I just mean that you got this."

Chapter 29

The New Era of Nati

Tonight I'm playing the first single of my yet-to-be-released EP. The album will be called *Nati*, to celebrate my first album as my real self. The hashtag #NewEraOfNati is ready to roll, a few of my fans with the biggest platforms ready to campaign for the new me.

In the cover art, I'm turned around—my curls falling down to the middle of my back—facing a purple background. It's going to be the style we go for with all the new singles. The palette, the serif font, everything.

I hold the phone with my hand, mesmerized.

It's perfect.

Alone in my dressing room, I practice slow breaths, trying to ease my mind. I do it from muscle memory—visualizing a large circle, each breath a line going clockwise. It takes me a moment to realize that I'm not as nervous as

I think. Or rather, I *am* nervous, but not like before. I don't miss my inhaler. Everything is easier when I'm owning being myself.

Someone knocks on my door. I have a brief flashback of what it was supposed to be like in the People's Choice Awards, the camera crew arriving at my dressing room to surprise me with the award of the evening, instead of surprising me backstage while Trent dumped me.

I chuckle, then catch myself. *Is that actually funny now?*

Opening the door, I find Bobbi on the other side, looking absolutely fabulous in a dark red business suit and matching dark red lipstick.

"Don't we look like twins," she teases, cocking an eyebrow and giving me a head-to-toe look.

"Absolutely," I say, adjusting my long red dress covered in sequins with a heart neckline. "You and I and everyone else here tonight. It is a Christmas special, after all."

She nods. "How are we feeling tonight, Ms. Headliner?"

I take a deep breath. "Happy. Proud." I shrug. "Terrified."

Bobbi laughs, then pulls me into a one-arm hug. "Listen, Nati, you'll be phenomenal. You've rehearsed more than any client I've ever had. Your new song is genuine and catchy, and it's going to top the charts."

"It's a big risk," I quote her without realizing. "Mixing Portuguese and English. Not many pop songs do that outside of Brazil."

She stares blankly at me. "So? You'll be the first. Start a legacy. Other Latinx singers have been doing it with Spanish for ages. It's time a Brazilian did it, too."

Her words put a little more weight on my shoulders than I think I can carry, but they also give me a much-needed confidence boost. Instead of trying to put into words what this means to me—how she's betting everything on this new era, along with me—I pull her in for a proper hug.

I think we both want to put it into words anyway, but neither of us can right now. If we try, we may end up messing up our makeup, and our makeup artists would not be happy with that.

For the benefit of the greater good, I pull back.

"Look at that cocky smile," she says. "Aren't you going to crush it tonight?"

I nod. "I am."

"Good." Bobbi lets me go, and takes a step back, her hand on the doorknob of the dressing room. "Because Kimmy Lopez is onstage now. You enter in five."

With that, she disappears, like a magical fairy godmother of the biz.

I stop in front of the mirror, straightening the front of my dress. My hair isn't *entirely* natural, but it's a TV version of my natural hair. The waves fall down my back, two little braids just over my ears connecting at the back of my head, dark and silky. I love that. I love that my fake eyelashes are so huge, and my eyelids are covered in glitter. I'm not wearing any contour, which makes me a *little* nervous. My nose isn't as thin and my cheekbones aren't as defined as my past performances would have you think, but hopefully the crowd will like what they see as much as I like it now.

I really, really do. I like it all.

I smile at myself.

Then I get my phone from the couch in the back of the room, and text three of the most important people I know.

TO "MOM"

going in. ready to start snapping pictures like the papz?

everyone knows that mom pics are the best pics

TO "VOVÓ"

oi, vovó!

i hope you & everyone can watch me on netflix

the stream has already started, i enter in five minutes!

:) beijinhos (if i spelled it wrong, i meant kisses)

TO "WILLIAM"

wish you were here

I stare at the screen for a long moment. Before any of them can reply, I set my phone on airplane mode, so the notifications will stop.

I'm ready.

Nothing can compare to being under lights so bright that you can't even see the crowd. You still hear it, though. You still feel it. The screams fill the arena with energy; everyone's vibrating on the same level, for the same thing—being part of something. Together.

I grab the mic from center stage and give the audience my widest grin. "Good evening, Los Angeles! I am Nati." The crowd roars, and I somehow feel it in my chest. All of me vibrates back. "I'm going to sing something new for you, all right? It's called 'Natal at Home.' *Natal* is '*Christmas*' in Portuguese, and this year will be the first time in years I spend it with all of my family there. It's a bit autobiographical, you know?" I pause, raising my eyebrows. The crowd's still screaming. I'm still beaming. "It's about acceptance and joy. Let's hope you like it!"

As the first notes start and I move across the stage, I try to make sure the entire arena feels like part of the moment. The spotlights are so strong and hot that I can't focus on a single face. But it's enough for now to feel them with me.

This is the first time I sing "Natal at Home" for an audience bigger than the one at the studio. Bigger than Mom and my best friends at home.

What I'd said before to Bobbi still stands: I'm terrified. And happy. And proud.

When I hit the second verse, I hear people's attempts to follow along. It brings tears to my eyes, but I swallow them down and keep singing.

By the time I reach the chorus, they've learned a good part of the song.

They're singing along.

Making an effort to say the words in Portuguese. Making an effort to learn about me, to participate in this journey. Perhaps I'm naïve—it's possible they just want to have a good time—but the energy I feel confirms it.

I throw a kiss to one of the cameras before the final verse.

When the song ends, the arena erupts into applause and screams.

I hear their attempts at saying my name. Some still call me *Natalie*. Some pronounce *Nati* wrong. But most of them are saying it right.

"Thank you, Los Angeles. You have been incredible. Happy holidays and Feliz Natal!" I bow down, and when I come back up, the smile is still plastered to my face; it feels like I'll be smiling forever.

The crowd is still chanting variations of my name when I turn around and jog backstage.

And I see him.

William.

Clapping for me.

My jogging slows, and I'm frozen.

He's wearing a beautiful suit and black oxfords, hair slicked back, and stupid superhero socks, the ones I gave him. His proud, beaming smile, his ... his face. His eyes are such a beautiful green, a spark of joy in them like I haven't seen in a while.

I missed him so, so much.

I take slow steps to him, a little unsure of how to proceed. I did send him a text saying I wished he were here, but I'd fully expected him to ignore that and not materialize within the next ten minutes in California.

"Hi," I say, because anything else would be asking too much of me.

He waits until I stop in front of him. "Hi."

Behind us, someone else starts singing a pop song and the crowd continues to scream.

He shifts his weight to the other foot. "Look, Nati—"

"William, I—" I stop myself. "Sorry, you can speak."

"No, I interrupted you." He shakes his head. "Go first."

We stare at each other for a solid second.

I chuckle, rolling my eyes, and he chuckles, too, his cheeks turning red.

"I ... love that you're here." I take a deep breath and a

tentative step in his direction. "But why are you here? Why now?"

He bites his lip. Is his hand shaking?

"Today is . . . it's officially day one."

I frown, parting my lips.

Three people from the crew run by us with microphones, but it's like we're invisible. The show goes on, and the crowd keeps cheering. I take the feedback earpiece off, as if I could have misheard him.

"Day one?" I raise my eyebrows.

He nods, looking like he did the first time we saw each other. Out of his element and shy, but also shining bright. "As of now, we're not contractually obligated to fake-date each other." He tilts his head up, taking a deep breath. "And I would love . . . I would love to take you out on a date. On a real date. Somewhere just the two of us."

My heart will probably break out of my rib cage at any moment now.

This is so, so difficult, but I force the words out anyway: "I want to say yes. But if you leave again in a few weeks when the next story of us comes out, it'll hurt so much more." Balling my fists, I glance away. "I'm still . . . me."

"I know," he says slowly, more quietly than before, and takes a step closer to me. "And I'm not going to lie, it'll take some getting used to. I value my privacy, I value my family's privacy. But I talked a lot with Cedrick about this . . ."

He takes my hands in his and looks me in the eye. "There are things we can do to be more careful—things *I* can do. Like keeping my social media off, since I don't like that anyway." William shrugs, and I offer him a small smile.

I'm still struck at our hands together. How much I've missed him and how well they fit.

"But there will always be paparazzi. Even if we're careful, and Ashley has our backs. Something else could still happen."

"And when it does, we'll handle it together." His hand squeezes mine, and I look back at those emerald-green eyes. "Not being with you is so incredibly hard. I don't think I want to go through that again if I can help it."

I bite back a smile, and raise my eyebrows. "Are you saying you can't live without me?"

He laughs, looking back at our hands like I'd been doing a moment before. "Something like that, yes." William pauses, his thumbs caressing the back of my hands, and then he brings them both closer to his face. Gently, he places a kiss on my knuckles, and my legs turn to jelly. Staring at me from under those long eyelashes, he asks, "So, Nati. Will you go on a date with me?"

I can't stop myself.

Without a word, I close the space between us, both hands on the front of his blazer, and pull him to me, until our lips crash. Urgent, hungry kisses that feel like both a homecoming and a new beginning.

He sweeps me off my feet, and the warmth in my chest spreads until I'm catching fire. I can feel his heart racing under my palm, and when he puts me down, I snuggle into his chest.

"Does that mean you'll add me to your diary?" he asks.

I nod. "I think I can make time for a date with you, yes."

He mirrors my smile. Still slightly crooked. His full lips slightly bruised from our kisses.

He touches his forehead to mine, and when our noses touch briefly, he says, "I missed you a lot, Nati." His voice is lower than before. I lean into his touch, when his hand cups my face. "You know I tried to stay away? But I couldn't. Everything reminded me of you way too much . . . all the time." He breathes out heavily, and I catch my bottom lip between my teeth. "I'm sorry it took me this long to come." His dark green eyes search mine.

I place my hand on his chest, then hold his face. I trace the birthmark on his cheek and smile. "It's okay. You're here now. And it's perfect, because it's real."

I wrap my arms around his neck and kiss him again.

Chapter 30

Natal at Home

"Are you afraid?" I ask William.

He looks me in the eye and pauses. I know what that pause means.

"It's okay to be afraid," I reassure him. "It's okay if you're scared."

William shakes his head. "I'm not—I'm not *scared*. I'm . . . reluctant about being at ease."

He is totally freaking out.

But I am the bigger person in this relationship, and I am not going to make fun of him for being scared of planes *even though he's been through this so many times before.*

I pull up the seat divider between us and lean into his embrace. He puts an arm around me, but his shoulders are stiff and he may or may not cut all blood flow in my arm with the way he's playing with one of my hair elastics.

I touch his hand so he stops. He's still holding his breath. Deer-in-the-headlights big green eyes. "I'm cool. Flying is cool." He shrugs, squeezing my shoulder gently. Then he looks away and adds, apparently more to himself than me, "Except there's nothing cool about defying gravity with an impossibly heavy metal thing floating around."

We both watch as William spreads his toes in his super-hero socks.

"I'm trying really hard not to make fun of you right now," I say.

He parts his lips, and I smile, closing my eyes and pressing my lips to his. It's a quick peck, but it awakens all the butterflies that have been going wild inside my stomach since he stepped foot in the United States. Or rather, since he literally swept me off my feet backstage after my big headlining number for the Christmas special.

"I have a theory . . . ," I begin.

He runs a hand down my curls, careful not to undo them, both absentminded and mesmerized. I like that distracted look on him. "Do tell, Nati."

"I think . . ." I take a deep breath. "That you're more nervous about meeting my family than you are about flying."

It's the elephant in the room—the elephant in first class—so I might as well address it. He looks dumbfounded, as if that'd never occurred him. He offers me an awkward chuckle.

"I'm—I'm not nervous. Not about your family.

They're—they seem like perfectly good people." He smiles with pressed lips, so much tension on his face that it's a wonder he's still functioning. "I'm—I'm *curious,* if anything. Not about your family, that sounded like they were exotic or something. No, I meant curious about Brazil?" William raises his eyebrows. "Brazil seems like a wonderful place."

"We're not sightseeing much." I shrug. "It's just Christmas with my family."

The plane jolts with a bit of turbulence. After a pause, he says, "And I'm very excited."

I follow his gaze to see Mom, in the next row over, fast asleep.

"Seriously?" I ask. He lifts his shoulders again. I roll my eyes, pulling away from him. "Mom's not going to hear if you trash-talk anything. Brazil, my relatives, Christmas and other Christian traditions, whatever." I smile. "Don't worry."

William's eyes widen. "Nati, I don't want to trash-talk any of that."

I laugh. "Okay. I know that, don't worry. But, like, is it okay that you're coming? I mean, I don't want you to feel pressured or anything. It's a little late to be asking, but—"

William takes my hand in his. Interlacing our fingers, he brings the back of my hand to his lips. That causes more than a little flutter in my stomach, but I bite back my smile so I can keep the conversation going.

"I'm so happy to be here," he says, in a tone that makes it sound like he's admitting a secret. "When you invited me to go to Brazil with you . . . that's more than meeting your family. I felt that was you asking me to go and fight your demons with you," he says, and when I tilt my head to the side, making a face, he's quick to add, "Your family is not the demon. The demons are your fears and insecurities about going back. That's what I meant. Just in case that wasn't clear."

I squeeze his hand. "It was." I come closer to him again, but stop before kissing him. "It means a lot to me that we can fight them together."

He nods, then his eyes lower to my lips. I feel that something-more-than-a-flutter strengthen. A smirk appears on my face as I back away just an inch, just as he was coming a little closer. He laughs and I laugh, and just when we're about to really kiss . . . someone clears their throat.

We untangle from each other. There's a girl about my age standing next to our seats, her phone in hand. "Hi, so sorry to interrupt. I really am. But . . . Nati, you're my hero!" Her eyes go to William. She's still smiling. "And I hope this isn't weird to say, but I'm so happy to see you guys together as well? You're totally my OTP."

I smirk at William. He's frowning, mouthing to me, "OTP?"

"One True Pairing. Favorite ship. Favorite couple," I explain. Then, with a wink, "Keep up, London boy."

He laughs, shaking his head. The girl in front of us looks like she may pass out.

"I was so scared you weren't together. . . . There was nothing on social media! And there always is," she says, clutching her phone like she could break it.

"We're on a bit of a social media cleanse. At least about our personal lives," I explain.

She nods, like she understands.

"But that doesn't mean I can't take a picture."

Her face lights up. William offers his hand so he can take the picture of us, and I start getting up. The girl gestures for me to wait, and after another beat she asks, "Would it be . . . okay . . . for all three of us to be in the selfie? It's not because you're Nati's boyfriend! That's how I first saw your movies, but . . . *Rendezvous* is now my favorite! I couldn't stop thinking about it. . . . And I'm so happy to see you're going to be in the next *The Picture of Dorian Gray* retelling!"

William parts his lips. My gorgeous boyfriend with his cheeks turning pink. His lips are pink, too. I want to kiss them.

He looks so damn proud of himself. And he deserves it. Deciding to steer clear of blockbusters and only pursue passion projects, even if they're mostly indie and don't make that much money, has been something he was always clearly headed toward, but it still took courage to decide upon.

I am proud of him. Taking ownership of his career, too. Just like me.

William grins. "I'm happy to hear that. I can't wait to start shooting come the new year. And, of course, I'd love for us to take a selfie together."

The girl jumps at that, letting out a little scream. Someone in the row hisses at the noise, since the lights are dimmed for sleeping. She composes herself, still smiling big. "Cool! I'll get in the frame, then."

She lowers herself so we can both stay seated. William's arm is around me and the fan's beaming grin is mirrored in the screen as she snaps a thousand pictures for the perfect one. When she's done, she seems so happy that I'm about to tear up as well.

"Thank you so much," she says, looking down at her phone. Then at me. "And I really love your shirt." She points. I'm wearing a white crop top with the words LATINA AF in red. "You two have a wonderful flight."

We wave goodbye. Then I turn to him.

"She couldn't stop thinking about you," I whisper.

He holds back, but I see that for what it is: He's about to *giggle.* "Well, you're her hero."

I hum. "Seems like all your fears came true, and we're a power couple."

William ponders that, then shrugs. "I guess I can live with that. But now, more importantly, where were we?" He taps open the map on seat back's screen.

I pull his face closer to mine, and before kissing him, I say, "Right where we're supposed to be."

Acknowledgments

Mamis, obrigada. Sem o teu apoio incondicional, eu não estaria aqui. Obrigada por acreditar em mim muito antes que eu pudesse acreditar em mim mesma. Todas as minhas vitórias são dedicadas à ti, hoje e sempre. Te amo.

I am so happy to say that *Like a Love Song* is a product of love from a Dream Team. Thank you so much to Chelsea Eberly, who I'm proud to call my agent, who saw the potential of this book at a pitching event and helped me shape it into something much more meaningful for submission. Thank you so much to Hannah Hill, my brilliant editor, who swooned with me on a video call and convinced me from the first minute that she was the perfect person to continue to shape this book into what you hold in your hands now. Also, have you *seen* that cover? I am so grateful for Casey Moses, the wonderful designer, and Erick Dávila, the wonderful illustrator, for this phenomenal job. I am never going to get over this beautiful cover. To the Delacorte/Underlined team, Wendy Loggia, Beverly Horowitz, Tamar Schwartz, Colleen Fellingham, Andrea Lau, Dominique Cimina, Elizabeth Ward, and John Adamo, you are truly magical.

This book wouldn't be the same without the never-ending support from Robin, Natasha, Vanshika, Elisa, Sofia, Ams, Priyanka, Mith, Joana, Adriano, Camila, Luma, Isa, and Lily. You have all held my hand through multiple manuscripts and this process too. I am forever grateful to you, friends.

A special thank-you to Adiba, the first person I asked, "What if I wrote a rom-com?" Thank you for being by my side through drafting pains and sub pains, always celebrating my victories. All the positive adjectives in the world can't describe you.

A major thank-you to book bloggers, librarians, and teachers. You're all the backbone of this society! I can never thank you enough, not only for supporting my book, but also for putting so many amazing books in my hands throughout the years.

I've been a teacher myself for a decade, and I want to thank my students for these wonderful years. I have a hard time thinking about our classes together without choking up. Thank you for inspiring me and for listening to me when I opened my heart, and for opening your hearts to me. I meant every word I said about how I know that each of you is going to change the world. I love you. I hope you never forget that. Titier ama vcs bbs.

Finally, thank you for giving this book a chance. It means the world to me.

ABOUT THE AUTHOR

Gabriela Martins is a Brazilian kidlit author and linguist. Her stories feature Brazilian characters finding themselves and finding love. She was a high school teacher and has also worked as a TED Ed-Club facilitator, where she helped teens develop their own talks in TED format. She edited and self-published *Keep Faith*, an LGBTQ+ anthology, with all profits going to queer people in need. When she's not writing, she can be found cuddling with her two cats or singing loudly and off-key. *Like a Love Song* is her debut novel.

gabrielawrites.com